THE LAST GOODBYE

A World War II Novella

SAMANTHA GROSSER

SAM GROSSER
BOOKS

THE LAST GOODBYE

Cover Design by ArtMishel

For my mother, whose stories inspired this novella.

Chapter One

EMMA

AUSTRALIA, 2014

It was late morning when Emma turned into the street where she used to live and saw the old apartment block unchanged, sun-bright and warm in the late summer heat. From beyond the houses across the road she could hear the murmur of the surf on the beach, mesmerising and full of memories of a happier time: the first flush of excitement of a new life in Sydney, the hope and expectation of new love. She stopped for a moment to listen, hoping to be soothed by the rhythmic shush-hush of the water. She should walk along the sand while she was here, she thought, in a last goodbye to a place she had thought for a while she would never leave. But the impulse slid away almost as soon as it had risen, and she walked on, making her way along the little walkway and up the stairs towards the flat that was no longer her home.

On the landing outside, she hesitated, the key hanging loosely between her fingers. Jamie had promised he would not be home, but still it seemed wrong not to knock, just in case. He might have forgotten she was coming. He might be inside, with one of the women who had brought about the end of their relationship. Emma suppressed a shiver at the thought of it, despite the warmth of the day. She knocked, knuckles rapping loudly on the wood. Nothing. She knocked again. If he had fallen asleep in the bedroom, he would not hear her. She pressed her ear to the door. No movement. No music. No TV. Letting out a long breath that did nothing to steady her racing heart, she slipped the key into the lock and opened the door.

The flat was exactly as she remembered it, except she was acutely aware that it was no longer her home. She let her eyes wander across the fraying sofa, the old wooden cupboard, the posters on the walls, the surfboards propped up in the corner, and realised there was nothing in the place of her at all. It was all Jamie: his furniture, his taste, his things. It was hard to believe she had ever lived here at all. Three years of her life, and all she would take from it would fit into the two sports bags in her hand.

Outside on the balcony, a cockatoo landed with a clatter on the rail and began to squawk. She watched it for a moment through the window, gathering her resolve. Then, finally, with a little lift of her shoulders and a deep breath, she headed through the bedroom to collect up the belongings she had not taken when she'd walked out of Jamie's life a few short weeks before.

Just before she left, she did a final sweep, casting one last look around the flat she had once adored. It seemed shabby to her now with its discoloured paint and thinning carpet, and there was nothing of her that remained within its walls. The ache she had felt at leaving began to ebb, but still she wanted to be gone, half expecting the familiar wash of loss to sweep through her again. Absently, she ran her fingertips across the kitchen counter and her eyes lit upon a little stack of post, propped against the coffee machine. She rifled through it. A couple of official-looking letters for Jamie that could have been traffic violations, a card for a long-departed previous tenant, and a slim white envelope addressed in neat black handwriting to her.

Emma frowned and turned it over between her fingers. In spite of the handwritten address, it had a legal air about it that sent a vague ripple of unease across her, an automatic sense of guilt for as yet unknown transgressions. Sliding an instinctive glance towards the open door, as though checking she was still alone, she tapped the letter against her fingers, considering. She wanted to be gone, half afraid of meeting Jamie and eager to put the whole business behind her, but the letter had roused her curiosity.

The sudden bang of a car door in the street outside startled Emma from her thoughts and, stuffing the envelope into the pocket of her jacket, she picked up her bags and walked out of the flat for the final time without a backward glance.

Later, she dropped the two bags onto the narrow bed in the little room in a down-at-heel shared flat that had been the best she could afford when she had ended it with Jamie. The usual taint of damp permeated the air and she opened the window with a shove, letting in the clamour of the street along with the afternoon breeze, the hubbub of voices from the café downstairs. Weary now from the day's emotions, she left the bags unpacked and wandered out to the kitchen. Waiting for the kettle to boil, she remembered about the letter and took it from her pocket, sliding a finger under the flap and coaxing it open.

The letterhead announced *Fenchurch, Woolacott and Partners, Solicitors, London*, and the same breath of guilty unease passed through her before her eyes skimmed down across the page, searching for the details – money she owed, a fine she had not paid, someone accusing her of something. So it took a moment for her to understand the actual words.

We are delighted to inform you that you are the sole beneficiary in the stated last will and testament of Isobel Landon, of Cherry Tree Cottage, Cavendish Lane, Little Sutton, Norfolk, United Kingdom.

We are instructed to distribute the financial assets of the estate to you, and to facilitate your travel to England to take possession of the house and effects at your earliest convenience.

There are a number of documents that require your signature – if you can email us at the above address at your earliest convenience, we will forward these to you forthwith.

We look forward very much to hearing from you ...

She read it again. And again, for a third time.

Bewilderment and disbelief tumbled in her thoughts. Who on earth was Isobel Landon? And why would she leave an inheritance for Emma? She trawled the confusion of her thoughts for a memory but the name rang no bells – there was no half-forgotten presence from her past, no vague sense she might have heard that name before. A long-lost relative, perhaps? She thought of her parents, and her grandparents, but there was no one still living she could ask. She shook her head against the bafflement, hoping to re-order her thoughts into some sort of sense. It made no difference.

She let the sheet of paper fall onto the kitchen counter and made the tea on automatic pilot, numb with shock. Then she sat at the table with her cup, and picked up the letter to peruse it again. It was a scam, she decided. It had to be. She was not the kind of person this sort of thing ever happened to.

But still ...

Getting up with a sigh, she took her cup to the sink. An inheritance would be nice, she thought, as she rinsed out the mug. It would be a way out of the doldrums her life had become since she and Jamie had broken up, a chance to start again, instead of this endless round of work and sleep to make ends meet and no money for anything else.

After she had left him, Emma had realised that Jamie had been her whole life. Her friends were his friends, her social world belonged to him, and everything she did revolved around him. When she had decided to stay in Australia to be with him at the end of her working holiday, she had simply moved into his life, lovestruck and swept away by the romance of the beaches where he spent his days in the surf. And by the time it was over, there was absolutely nothing left in her life of her own. Without him, Emma had abruptly found herself friendless and alone.

She turned from the sink and rested her hips against it, looking once more at the letter that lay on the table. It looked official, she thought. The English was correct and plausible, and they hadn't asked for any money, requesting only that she email them. For a moment she hesitated, caught between curiosity and scepticism. What did she have to lose? An email couldn't hurt, surely?

Sitting down again at the table, she reached for her laptop and opened it, waiting with the usual slight sense of trepidation as it whirred reluctantly into life. But the little flourish eventually announced the computer's continuing health, and she opened up her email and started to type.

Chapter Two

EMMA

England, 2014

It was not a scam, and in what seemed like no time at all Emma had finished up her life in Sydney and was on her way back to England to start afresh. But in all the correspondence with the solicitor she had found out nothing more about the mysterious Isobel Landon, and the not knowing kept her awake at night, turning over the endless possibilities in her mind, all of them unlikely, impossible, and in the sleepless early hours she half expected to wake to the news that it was all a mistake – she was the wrong person after all, and the inheritance belonged to someone else.

But each morning she woke up a little more used to the idea, a little more accepting of the fact that she was the owner of a cottage in Norfolk, that her bank account was full enough to make her very comfortably off. Slowly, shock gave way to delight. Perhaps she would find out more when she got to Little Sutton, she thought. Perhaps people in the village would be able to help. Smiling to herself, she looked out of the little aircraft window at the spectacular dwindling view of Sydney harbour, and settled in for the flight.

When Emma finally stepped off the bus in Little Sutton at the end of her journey it was late in the afternoon, and the shadows were growing long across the high street. She stood on the kerb and watched the bus pull away with a lurch, breathing deeply to calm the sudden rush of nerves as a new and unexpected life opened up in front of her. Australia already felt like another world, a different time and place. Had she ever really lived there? It seemed impossible now. It had been surprisingly easy to leave and, in the shock and excitement of it all, the last weeks had slipped past her barely noticed. There had been a hurried farewell for her at work, and they had given her an enormous bunch of flowers she had been sorry to leave behind in the hotel. Then the seemingly endless journey, her life suspended 30,000 feet above the earth, sleepless and still surprised to find herself there. She felt as though she were balanced on a narrow bridge between her past and her future, the present hazy and unreal, a blur of moving and travel, everything fleeting and transient.

Now, standing in the high street of Little Sutton with the two suitcases that were all she had brought from Sydney, her whole past life packed inside them, she cast her gaze across the village. Pretty stone cottages lined either side of a wide street that boasted a pub, a village shop and a hairdresser. In the distance she could see the tower of a church that was set off the road a little way, the stone walls lit with a golden hue in the afternoon sun. There was no one about – it was the lull between the afternoon and evening when people were at home, preparing dinner, and the shop sign was already turned to *CLOSED*. She thought of the supermarkets in Sydney, open all hours, and gave herself a wry smile. She would need to be a little more organised with her shopping now.

Reaching into the pocket of her jacket, she drew out the folded sheet of paper with the address – even though the address was firmly lodged in her mind, the note was worn thin with handling, her need for tangible proof of it.

Cherry Tree Cottage, Cavendish Lane, Little Sutton, Norfolk.

The road was easy to find – a turning off the high street just before the church – and at the corner she stopped to square her shoulders, uncertain what she might find. But when she turned into the lane she let out the breath she hadn't realised she was holding with a great sigh of pleasure. A little row of neat stone cottages was half hidden by pretty gardens that were bright with a profusion of hyacinths and irises, tulips and narcissi. Fruit trees stretched their branches atop the hedges, pink with blossom, and all the uncertainty about what she would find at the end of her journey gave way to sudden excitement as she hurried along the lane, the wheels on the suitcases catching on the uneven ground. She checked off each house in turn as she passed them.

Apple Tree Cottage, Plum Tree Cottage, and, at the far end of the row her own house, complete with a cherry tree in front, the verge beneath it dotted pink with fallen petals.

Emma halted at the low wooden gate and looked it over.

Her house. Her very own house. She still struggled to believe it and she could feel her heart as it pattered in her chest, her mouth was dry with anticipation, still half expecting someone to come along and tell her it was all a mistake, that the cottage wasn't hers after all. Quickly now, eager, she shoved open the gate, dragged the cases up the path and, after fumbling in her bag for a moment of panic before her fingers closed on the key, she opened the door and stepped inside.

The door opened into a cosy living room with a kitchen beyond it. An open fireplace took up most of one wall – she would have to learn how to set a fire, she thought. In front of her, a narrow staircase led up to the first floor. Putting down the cases she hesitated, still caught in the disbelief that the place was really hers, assailed by a sense that she was trespassing. She cast her gaze across the room, Isobel Landon's presence still lingering in the furnishings and paintings on the walls, the ornaments along the mantelpiece, a stack of unopened letters on the kitchen counter. It would take time, Emma guessed, to make the place properly her own and feel at home there.

Still uncertain, she took a step forward and ran her fingertips along the back of the sofa. It was a good piece of furniture, covered in soft green velvet with cushions of russet-red propped against the arms: old-fashioned but tasteful. Inviting. Emma kicked off her shoes and went to the fireplace, toes curling into the softness of an Afghan rug as she ran her eyes across the cluttered mantelpiece above it. In among the trinkets – a lapis lazuli Buddha, a tiny Eiffel Tower, figurines of jade and porcelain – two small photographs were nestled in pretty silver frames. They were both black-and-white, tinted with sepia, and they looked to Emma as though they might be from the 1940s.

She picked up first one then the other. The first was of a young woman with intense bright eyes and a sweep of blonde hair that gave her a look of a young Lauren Bacall. Her lips were upturned just slightly at the corners, as though she were suppressing a smile. Emma smiled in return then turned the picture over, hoping for some information on the back. But there was nothing written and she was reluctant to take the photograph out of its frame just yet. It looked so right there, so comfortable.

'Are you Isobel?' Emma murmured. Perhaps, she thought, and hoped so. It was good to have a face to put to the name – it gave her benefactor a more tangible presence.

The other picture was of a young man in what she assumed was an American uniform, although she couldn't be certain. He was handsome, with sad dark eyes and black hair that was just beginning to curl on the ends in spite of the shortness of his haircut. There was no smile on his lips, which gave him a serious air, and she touched her fingertips to the glass, tracing the lines of his face.

'Who are you?' she asked the picture. 'And where do you fit into the story?'

Tucking the photograph carefully back in its place, she turned and went through to the kitchen. It was clean and bright and surprisingly modern, with marble worktops and a terracotta tile floor. A small table stood against the wall, and the refrigerator hummed with life. The solicitor had assured her that all the services were still connected, and she need only transfer them to her own name.

Idly, she opened the fridge. It was empty of course, and she smiled at herself, realising she had been hoping to find milk for tea. Checking all the other cupboards, she found them well stocked with unopened packets of rice and tea and pasta, jars of jam and local honey, cans of tomatoes and beans. There were pots and pans aplenty and a pretty set of crockery with some kind of willow design – everything she could possibly need in a kitchen was there.

She went upstairs. There were two small bedrooms – one with a double bed that had been stripped of its linen, and the other with a sofa bed and desk beneath a window that looked out over the garden behind the house and the churchyard beyond. It was a lovely view, the perfect place for a desk. She found some linen, neatly folded in a closet on the tiny landing, sweetly scented with lavender. Taking it through to the bedroom, she made up the bed, then stood back with a smile.

She was home.

In the evening she went to the pub in the high street for dinner, stepping warily into the lane in the country dark, nervous about her reception in the village. Would the villagers know who she was? Were they expecting her? Little Sutton was a tiny place –

she was certain everyone knew everyone's business, and she was not quite sure how she felt about that. She was used to the anonymity of living in a city.

The Golden Lion was only a few minutes' walk away, and the warm scent of beer and pub food drifted out to the street before she even opened the door, welcoming. Outside on the footpath she paused a moment, gathering her courage – it had been a long time since she had gone into a pub alone, a long time since she had even socialised. In the months since she and Jamie had parted, she had barely done anything other than work and sleep. Now, her breathing was quick and shallow with nerves, and her mouth was dry as she straightened her shoulders and forced herself to take a couple of long deep breaths, her courage faltering. What if they hated her? What if they refused to accept her? She shook her head against the possibility – this was her home now, and she could not hide away. With another deep breath and a ripple of resolve, she pushed open the door and went inside.

From the doorway she cast a quick look around. It was a cosy, old-fashioned place with a large hearth that she imagined would be welcome on winter nights, and plain wooden tables, old-fashioned hunting prints on tobacco-stained walls. It was empty except for two elderly men with half-pints and a sheepdog at their feet. They paid her no attention but the barman looked up from the glass he was polishing, and nodded a greeting. She nodded back and went to the bar.

'Evening,' the barman said. 'What can I get you?'

'A half of best, please.' She had planned to have a glass of wine, but old habits kicked in when she saw the gleaming brass beer pumps. It had been far too long since she had drunk English beer. 'And do you do food?'

'We do,' he replied. 'There's a menu on the chalkboard. Nothing fancy, but good enough.'

'I don't need fancy,' she answered, flicking a glance towards the chalkboard. 'I'm just hungry. What do you recommend?'

He smiled. 'Personally, I like the steak and stout pie.'

'Perfect. I'll have one of those please.'

He passed her beer across the bar and ducked out of sight towards the kitchen to see about her food. She settled herself on a bar stool and took a sip of her beer. It was cool and bitter and reminded her of student days, before she set off on her travels.

'Passing through, are you?' the barman asked when he returned. He was a middle-aged man with a tired smile and kind eyes.

'I've come here to live,' she replied, with a hopeful smile. 'I've inherited Isobel Landon's cottage in Cavendish Lane, though I don't know why. So it's a new start for me.' She looked up from her beer. 'Did you know her?'

'Everyone knows everyone here.' He lifted his eyebrows and Emma smiled. 'But Isobel was a very private soul. She wasn't standoffish or anything – she was very friendly – but she didn't talk about herself much. I don't think anyone really knew much about her.'

'Oh.' Emma let out a sigh of disappointment. She had been hoping for a different answer.

'You can ask around, of course. She might have shared a bit more with other people.'

'I'll do that. Thank you. My name is Emma, by the way.'

'Clive. Good to meet you. Welcome to Little Sutton.'

She smiled and took another mouthful of beer, her nerves beginning to ebb with his friendliness. It boded well.

When her pie arrived she went to sit at one of the tables by the empty fireplace. The elderly men with the sheepdog left, and for a while she was the only customer. She had just finished her meal and was thinking she should probably go home when the door opened again with a ring of its bell. Instinctively, she looked up at the sound and saw a man in his early thirties, about her own age, with dark hair and light lively eyes that lit on her imme-diately. He gave her an automatic smile which she returned before he turned his head away and crossed to the bar. With nothing else to occupy her, Emma watched as the newcomer chatted to Clive and, though she could not quite hear their words, it was clear they knew each other well. Then, with his freshly poured pint in his hand, he turned abruptly towards her and she dropped her eyes away, embarrassed to be caught watching him.

He approached her table. 'Do you mind if I join you?' he asked. 'Only there's nowhere else to sit.' He gave a little shrug, casting a look around the empty pub, and she laughed.

'Well, in that case, it would be unkind of me to say no.'

He slid onto the stool across from her and held out his hand. 'Andrew Norton. Andy. I live at Apple Tree Cottage, two doors along from you. Clive said you've moved into Isobel's place? That makes us neighbours.'

She took his hand and shook it. A warm, firm grip briefly encircled her own small hand. 'Emma Moss. It's nice to meet you.' She smiled. 'Yes. It's all rather strange about the cottage. I didn't know her. I didn't even know she existed. To be honest, I'm still in a bit of a state of shock. Did you know her well?'

He took a mouthful of beer then licked the foam from his upper lip with the tip of his tongue. He was rather nice, she thought, and the total opposite of Jamie. Clean-cut, eager, no attitude, no effort to be cool. Already, she liked him.

'I knew her a bit,' he said. 'I'm the local community nurse around here and so I spent quite a bit of time with her, especially towards the end.' He had a faint lilt to his tone, the remnants of an Irish accent. It gave his voice a pleasant softness.

'Was she very ill?'

'She got quite weak so she needed help to mobilise and with her medications … dying is never pretty but she was quite sanguine about it, said she'd lived a good life and it was her time to go.'

'Did she mention me at all? Why she would leave everything to me?'

He shook his head. 'She talked a little bit about her past in the last few weeks. She was a photographer. Travelled all over the world – went to some dangerous places, worked for different newspapers, magazines.' He gave a little shrug. 'I don't know much more than that, I'm afraid.'

'No family?'

'Not that she ever mentioned to me.'

'Hmm.' Emma sat back. 'It's a mystery.'

'Indeed. Although you might find something at the house, I suppose. Old letters, diaries. I don't suppose you've had a chance to look yet, but I'd wager there's a stash of old stuff lying around somewhere. You don't get to be eighty-eight without collecting some memorabilia.'

'There are a couple of photographs on the mantelpiece.' She raised her eyebrows in question.

'Ah yes,' he remembered. 'She did tell me about those. One of them is her, during the war before she joined up with the Women's Air Force. Absolute stunner, wasn't she? And the other was an airman who was her "fancy-man" for a while, she said. I asked what happened to him but that's all she would tell me. Sorry. I'm not being very helpful, am I?'

'Yes, you are,' she contradicted him. 'You've told me loads.'

He finished his pint and pointed to her own empty glass. 'Another?'

Emma hesitated. She had planned to have an early night, exhausted from the travelling and the stress of moving conti-nents. But Andy was very good company and it was her first night in her new home, so she found herself nodding instead. 'Half of best, please.'

When he sat down again with the drinks she forced her mind away from her own concerns. 'Have you lived here long?' she asked.

'A couple of years. I used to live in London. I worked in a big hospital but I got tired of the stress, fancied a change. The job came up so I thought, why not? So here I am.'

'Do you like it here?'

'I do,' he smiled. 'The pace takes a bit of getting used to and you'll need a car to get around but it's a good life. Where were you living before?'

'Sydney.'

He lifted his eyebrows, impressed. 'Did you like it there? I've always wanted to go.'

'Yes,' she said. 'And no.'

He laughed.

'It's a beautiful city and the weather is gorgeous, but my life took a bit of a wrong turn while I was there, so it was actually good to leave. Fresh start and all that.'

'I can drink to that,' he answered, and lifted his glass. She raised hers and they clinked.

'Fresh starts,' they said, in unison, and laughed.

Later, they walked back to Cavendish Lane together and said goodbye at the gate of Apple Tree Cottage.

'I'll see you around,' he said. 'If you need anything, you know where I am.'

'Thanks. Good night,' she replied, and walked on to her own house.

Inside, she shrugged off her coat and hung it on the hook on the back of the door. Then she went to the mantelpiece and took down the little photo of the airman, wondering if he held the key to the mystery, or if he could at least set her on the right path.

Taking the picture to the kitchen where the light was brighter, she searched the drawers for a sharp knife. The frame was taped at the back, and when she found a little paring knife she slid the point along the joins and carefully teased the backboard away.

Afraid the photo had been glued to the board, she was delighted when it peeled away easily in her fingers. Holding her breath, she turned it over.

My darling Matthew, she read. *January 1944.*

She ran her fingertips across the words, tracing the old-fashioned script, the ink beginning to blur at its edges.

Matthew, she thought, and turned the picture over again to look at his face. He was very young, she realised. Twenty years old, perhaps? Not much more than that. He gazed at her intently, his eyes almost black in their darkness, his skin pale, his hair combed and neat. She gave him a small smile and slid the picture back into the frame to keep it safe. She would need to find tape tomorrow, she thought, and felt a wash of guilt at having disturbed him. But now she had a name at least. A connection, a path to follow.

Propping him gently back in his place on the mantelpiece she gave Isobel's image a nod goodnight, turned out the downstairs light and went upstairs to spend her first night in her new home.

Chapter Three

EMMA

Emma came across the diary quite by chance.

She had been living at Cherry Tree Cottage for a couple of months and was beginning to settle into her new life in Little Sutton. She had found a part-time job in the neighbouring town teaching English to migrants, and bought a small second-hand car, which she loved. She had made a start clearing out the cupboards and drawers to make space for her own things, and there was already a stack of boxes in the spare room packed with Isobel's clothes ready for the charity shop.

Every so often she bumped into Andy in the lane as they came and went, and they talked for a while in the way of neighbours, but they didn't go for a drink again and, for all that she liked him, a part of her was relieved – it was far too soon after Jamie to be thinking about someone new, her heart still raw and untrusting. She needed to make her own life, alone for a while, and find the strength in her independence. Then and only then, she had decided, would she think about starting to look for love again.

Still, seeing him always lifted her spirits. He was funny and kind, and they always parted with his offer that if she needed help with anything at all, she knew where he was. She met the people that lived in the cottage between them – a young couple who were friendly enough but kept themselves to themselves – and she had made friends with a couple of women from work, going out for a drink in town with them once or twice.

In her free time Emma did what she could to find out more about Isobel Landon. Who was this mysterious woman who had left Emma everything she owned? And what was the connection between them? She searched on the internet and enquired at the library in town. She went through all the likely places in the cottage where she might find notebooks or old letters, documentation of some kind, and although she found assorted correspondence from various friends and acquaintances dated in the last few years, along with old passports and bills, there was nothing that gave any clue to a link that stretched from Isobel to her.

But on a sunny afternoon towards the end of June, on a day that could not have been more perfect, she ventured for the first time into the shed at the end of the overgrown garden, using all her strength to drag open the door across the unmown grass. A cloud of dust threatened to make her cough; inside, spider webs hung in the corners, a row of dead flies littering the little windowsill. But the garden tools were stacked neatly in a rack along one wall and the shelves were orderly – a couple of toolboxes, containers of bits and pieces – gardening gloves and rolls of twine, bottles of weedkiller and fertiliser, plant pots and seedling trays, a straw hat and a bottle of sunscreen. Emma had never had her own garden before, and though this one was somewhat overgrown with weeds it was still quite beautiful with its flowering fruit trees and azaleas, and an aromatic bed of herbs against the wall that scented the air whenever she brushed past them.

She was looking for a trowel or a weeding tool, planning to

make a start on the rampant dandelions, and as she rummaged among the bits and pieces, casting her eyes across the shelves, her gaze landed on an old square biscuit tin, tucked away high on the top shelf, half hidden behind a row of empty glass jars and bottles. She couldn't have said why it drew her attention any more than any of the other boxes, except perhaps for the splash of colour it offered among all the greys and greens and browns. But it seemed out of place somehow, as though it had been placed there as an afterthought.

She considered it for a moment, reluctant to get distracted from the job in hand, and briefly she looked away, still running her eyes across the shelves, searching for a trowel. But the tin caught at the corner of her vision, insistent, and so, with a sigh for the dandelions, she stood on her toes to reach up and coax the tin towards her with her fingertips. When it was finally in her hands, she could feel the anticipation welling inside her, a sense of excitement, even as she told herself it was nothing, just another box of nails or screws or some such thing. She stood holding it in the dim light of the shed, the metal cool against her palms as she examined the faded colours on the lid – a royal crest and the name *Huntley & Palmers* in white lettering. Then she took it out into the garden where the light was brighter, and sat on the overgrown grass in the shade of the lilac tree to open it, tucking her fingers under the lid and working to prise it free. It opened abruptly with a snap, and when she saw the contents she gasped.

A leatherbound notebook. Photographs. A locket. A curl of a child's hair tied with a ribbon.

Emma swallowed, heart hammering, and looked up as though to check if anyone was watching. Two butterflies danced past her, the sun catching the vibrant colours of their wings, but otherwise she was quite alone. Hurriedly placing the tin on the ground beside her, eager now, she lifted the cover of the notebook and peered at the first page.

Isobel Landon, she read.

Little Sutton, January 1944.

It was the same writing as the back of the photograph. A diary? Emma's heart skipped a beat.

She should open it inside, she thought then. In case the book was fragile. In case it crumbled in her fingers and the breeze caught the pieces and blew them away. So, replacing the lid with care, she took the precious tin inside and put on the kettle for tea. Then she sat herself down at the kitchen table, took out the notebook and began to read.

Chapter Four

ISOBEL

Autumn 1944

This year has been a year of wonders – unexpected love, death, hope, new beginnings, and I hardly know where to start to record it. I only know I must, so that I don't forget a single detail in the years ahead. I kept notes through it all, though the exact dates are already a little hazy. But I suppose now is as good a time as any to set it all down in the proper order.

What I'll do with it once it's written, who can say?

January 1944

There were airmen in the shop again. There's nothing unusual about that, of course – the village is always full of them – although why they would come to Mrs Mackie's when they have their own well-stocked store of American provisions on the base is beyond me to imagine. There is so very little to buy here, with all the rationing. Sometimes they might buy a paper or a magazine, or one of the ancient faded postcards to send home, but I suppose that mostly they just come to look around, for a change of scenery.

Two days ago a whole group of them burst in through the door. I remember shivering with the rush of cold air that came in with them and the crazy tinkle of the bell as the door juddered with the force. One of them shot me a mock grimace of apology, which made me smile, but Mrs Mackie let out a loud sigh of irritation. She resents the airmen filling up her shop with their accents and their laughter and spending no money. I could hear her mumbling under her breath as she retreated to the back of the shop out of their way. I stood at the counter, watching them fool about, until one of them approached. He seemed quieter than the others, who were still larking around by the door, closing it with exaggerated care and pretending to walk on tiptoe, laughter barely suppressed. I flicked a glance towards the back of the shop – Mrs Mackie would ask them to leave if they carried on too much.

'I'm sorry about my friends,' the airman said. 'High spirits, you know?'

He took off his cap and turned it lightly over and over in his fingers. His hair was almost black and his dark eyes searched my face, as if he hoped to find understanding.

I smiled. 'I know.'

'I'm not sure your boss does, though.' He slid a look towards Mrs Mackie.

'No. I think you might be right about that.'

He smiled and did not turn away as I expected. The others, aware they had outstayed their welcome, opened up the door again, so gently this time the bell did not even quiver, and spilled out into the winter afternoon.

'Can I get you anything?' I asked.

The airman shook his head, but he did not follow his friends out of the shop and I was glad. I wanted him to stay. I wanted his dark gaze to remain on my face.

'Are you on a pass?' I asked.

'Not really. Just a free couple of hours between classes. They like to keep us busy.'

'You have classes?' I was surprised. I hadn't thought of the airmen as students – I had assumed they arrived fully trained, ready.

'All the time. Even the old hands. Things change – new technology, new dangers, new situations, new ways of doing things.'

'Of course. I didn't think.' Then, because I didn't want the conversation to end, I said, 'Are you an old hand?' It didn't seem likely. He was too young, not much older than me, I guessed. Twenty perhaps? Twenty-one? But anything was possible in war – for all I knew he had already been flying for years.

'Me?' He laughed, and his whole face lit up, lines crinkling at the corners of his eyes, mouth open wide. He was really very handsome, I thought. Beyond the glamour of the uniform and the allure of the foreign that made all the airmen seem attractive, there was something very sweet about him, a kindness in his eyes, a glint of mischief. 'No, not me. I just got here. I'm a rookie. Still training. Just flying around Norfolk, learning the ropes.'

The lightness seemed to leave us both, abruptly, as though an unexpected cloud had covered the sun, and I shivered.

'You're cold,' he said.

'I'm fine,' I answered quickly. But I wasn't fine. I was thinking of all the missions he had yet to fly, his first taste of war still to come, and I couldn't imagine how he could be so light-hearted in the face of it. In the village we knew better than most about the losses the fliers sustained. We watched them take off with the dawn each morning, rattling our doors and our windowpanes in their wake, deafening, and we counted them home in the afternoon. We saw the holes and the twisted broken metal, the engines that were broken and smoking, the planes that had to belly-land because the landing gear was all shot up. And we knew how many of the Fortresses failed to return at all, their crews either dead or on the run in Europe, or captured and in a PoW camp.

'My father is a flier,' I told him, though I hadn't planned to. I suppose I thought it would be a connection between us. He was easy to talk to – I felt none of the awkwardness I had always felt before in the presence of a man I liked. 'Or was. He's a prisoner of war now in Germany somewhere. Stalag Luft something …. We get letters now and then, but most of what he writes is blacked out by the censor. He flew Halifaxes …' I trailed off, uncertain what I was trying to say.

'I'm sorry to hear that,' the airman said.

There was a pause. We could hear Mrs Mackie shifting boxes in the back room, grunting with the effort and grumbling. We exchanged a small smile.

'I should probably go,' he said. 'My friends will be waiting.' He glanced towards the door but he didn't move, still turning the cap in his fingers.

Then he said, 'My name is Matt. Matthew Turner.' He gave me a hopeful smile, boyish and uncertain.

'Isobel Landon,' I replied.

We shook hands and his palms were warm and dry against my cold fingers, his grip strong but gentle. We let go of each other with reluctance and Matt dropped his eyes away, made shy by the pleasure in the touch of our hands. Then we stood for a moment with the counter between us, neither knowing what to say next.

Mrs Mackie's footsteps broke the moment, and he stepped quickly back and away.

'I'm here every day,' I whispered. 'Every day except Sunday for the next couple of weeks.

He nodded, flashed me a brilliant smile, and then with a merry tinkle of the bell on the door he was gone.

Chapter Five

EMMA

England, 2014

Emma closed the diary, willing herself not to read ahead, to search for her own part in the story. She was sure it would be there, somehow, the answer to the mystery. But now that it was in front of her she realised she was in no hurry to find it. She wanted to savour it and let the story unfold in its own time, as Isobel had intended.

She hadn't known that Little Sutton had hosted an airbase in the war. The librarian in town had mentioned that the area had been full of airfields, that the Americans had flown their raids in the daytime and the RAF had flown at night. But Emma hadn't thought about just how much all those airmen would have changed the lives of the villagers hereabouts. It must have seemed like an invasion of a sort. These villages had slumbered unchanged for centuries, generations of families working the same land undisturbed by the world outside their borders. No wonder Mrs Mackie had sighed and grumbled.

It was easy for Emma to picture it – the same shop where she bought her milk and bread, perhaps even the same bell on the door. Any changes the airmen had brought would not have lasted long after they left, she guessed. Old habits die hard, her mother used to say. She imagined the old ways had quickly reasserted themselves in the post-war years while England struggled through shortages and more rationing.

She had just put on the kettle for another cuppa when a knock at the door made her jump. Her pulse quickened in surprise. In all the weeks she had lived at the cottage not one person had ever visited, and she paused to run her fingers through her hair and smooth down her shirt before she moved across the living room towards the door.

Andy was on the doorstep, a sheepish smile on his face.

'Sorry to bother you on a Saturday afternoon, but I was wondering if you had any milk I could borrow? Only the shop's not open, and I completely forgot …'

She laughed, delighted to see him. 'Of course! Come in.'

He followed her into the cottage.

'I was just making some tea if you'd like some?' The automatic reflex to offer overcame her hesitation. Besides, she wanted to tell him about the diary.

'Thanks,' he replied. 'That would be grand.'

He sat at the kitchen table, and as she took out another mug from the cupboard, she said, 'Look at what's on the table. I found it in the shed this afternoon.'

Andy drew the tin towards him and lifted out the photos she had not even looked at yet.

'I started reading the diary,' she told him. 'It's from the war, when she was young. She just met her airman …'

Andy looked up at her with a smile of pleasure. 'That's fantastic! What about these?'

She dragged her chair round to sit beside him and they went

through the photographs together. Sepia, faded, and mostly unlabelled, they were of unknown families and children. They passed them hand to hand in silence, studying the faces of these unknown people, long dead, wondering. Only one of the pictures had a name on the back of it. It was a studio portrait of a baby in a pale knitted cardigan and little booties, a ribbon tied in the wispy blonde hair. She must have been about a year old when the picture was taken, Emma guessed, and she was looking at the camera with a wide-open gaze of interest, a chubby face that glowed with health.

'Cute!' Andy said, and turned the picture over.

Angela, 1945 was written in blurred black ink across the back, printed for clarity, and it was hard to say if it was the same hand that had written Matthew's name on his portrait.

'My mother's name was Angela,' Emma murmured, startled at the coincidence. 'She was born in 1944. She would have been about that age …'

'Why would Isobel Landon have a photograph of your mother?'

'I don't know, but perhaps that's where the connection is, somehow. Perhaps Isobel knew my grandmother?' They looked at each other, baffled, still struggling to make sense of the link. 'It's possible.'

'Does she look like your mum?' He tilted the photograph to the light so Emma could see it more clearly.

'Not how I remember her,' Emma said, and made a face. An unwelcome memory flickered through her thoughts – her mother's last days when there was almost nothing left of the woman Emma had loved. She closed her mind against it, calling up instead a happier, childhood image, her mother still healthy and laughing.

'Well of course,' Andy laughed. 'But you must have seen baby photos, pictures from when she was a child?'

Emma thought about it for a moment. 'Actually, no,' she said. 'I can't recall ever seeing pictures of my mother as a child. Or of my dad, come to that. But that's probably because he left when I was young and I never really knew him. Mum rarely talked about him. It was almost like he'd never existed.'

'That can't have been fun.'

'It's just how it was. It wasn't so bad. But I was happy to get away to university. Then I worked for a while to save up some money and then I travelled. Far, far away.' She paused. 'I didn't see her again. I was in Thailand when she died – it was all very quick and by the time I got back it was over.' She shrugged and gave him a rueful smile.

He gave her a small smile in return and returned his gaze to the photograph. 'I'm sorry to hear that. But this *could* be her ...'

'Yes,' she agreed, 'it could.' She reached and took the picture from him, examining the little face, searching for hints of her mother, but it was impossible to tell and after a while she set it back into the tin along with the others.

'I guess you'll just have to keep reading the diary,' he said.

She nodded and brushed the leather cover with her fingertips lightly.

'But not now,' Andy went on. 'I've been very remiss as a neighbour, and I think we should have dinner at the pub tonight. There's a local jazz trio playing, and I can introduce you to a few people. What do you say?'

'Well ...' The old hesitation rippled through her, her pleasure in his company tempered by a reluctance to get hurt again. Her heart still ached, a physical pain, and though Andy would never need to know, the sting of her humiliation at Jamie's hands could still bring a flush to her cheeks.

'Why not? What are you going to do instead?'

'Read the diary.'

'It'll keep,' he persisted. 'Go on. Live a little. It's Saturday night.

I'm buying.' He nudged his shoulder into her arm and she laughed.

'All right. You win.'

'Perfect. Seven o'clock? In the lane?'

She nodded. Then she got up to pour some milk into a jug for him to take home, and wished him goodbye, glad she had accepted.

Chapter Six

EMMA

England, 2014

The pub was starting to get busy when they arrived, and though the trio had not yet started their set, Emma could hear strains of soft jazz from the sound system, just audible above the chatter. It seemed a very different place from the quiet bar she had been to on her first night, buzzing now with anticipation.

They ordered beer and fish and chips at the bar then settled at a table in the corner. Andy pointed out people from the village she had not yet met. An elderly lady in a purple hat and red lipstick smiled and lifted a hand in greeting when she saw them looking her way.

'Who's that?' Emma asked. She seemed like an interesting character, with her neat cropped hair and perfect make-up. She must have been stunning in her youth.

'Ruby Simmons,' Andy answered. 'She and Isobel were friends. You should talk to her. She might be able to help.'

They took their drinks and went to sit at the old lady's table.

'Ruby, this is Emma.' Andy introduced them. 'Emma, Ruby.'

The two women gave each other a friendly smile.

'Isobel left Emma the cottage and we're still trying to work out why. You wouldn't know anything about it, would you?'

Ruby gave a quick shake of her head.

'She must have said something.' Andy tried again. 'Anything.'

Ruby took a sip from her bottle of pale ale and regarded Emma across the top of it with blue eyes that were surprisingly clear.

'Izzy played her cards close to her chest,' she said, after a moment of consideration. 'I always thought she had some great sadness locked inside, a shameful secret, or something in her past she couldn't face. She lost the love of her life in the war, but you probably know that. Matthew. She had his picture on the mantelpiece.'

'It's still there,' Emma said, 'next to the one of Isobel. I couldn't bear to take them down. They're such a handsome couple.'

Ruby nodded. 'She was always something of a beauty with that hair and her boyish figure.'

'Did you know her when she was young? Did you grow up here too?' Emma was excited to have found someone who might be able to help, someone who had known Isobel for a long time.

'She was older than me by a few years, but I remember her,' Ruby said. 'She used to work in the shop in the war and if Mrs Mackie wasn't looking she'd throw a couple of extra lemon sherbets or a barley sugar above the ration into the bag for us kids. We used to time our visits to make sure she'd be there.' Ruby smiled with the recollection. 'Then when she finished school she joined up with the WAAF and left the village.' She stopped, realising the acronym was no longer familiar to most people. 'The Women's Auxiliary Air Force,' she clarified. 'Everyone was surprised – she was destined for university – top of her class all through school. But I expect she had her reasons. Probably wanted to do her bit, like the rest of us.' She paused and took a mouthful of her drink. 'I didn't see her for years after that. I heard she went to Belgium with the forces after the war, but that's all. And after a while, people forgot about her. Her parents moved away – her father was in the air force too – and so it was a wonderful surprise when she bought Cherry Tree Cottage and moved back a few years ago. You could have knocked me down with a feather. I reckon I was the only one left that remembered her but she hadn't really changed much, still the same kind soul, the same sense of mischief.'

'Did she tell you what she'd been doing all those years?' Andy asked. He seemed as interested to know as Emma. But then, he had known Isobel in her final years and Emma felt a pang of envy that she had never met this remarkable woman.

'Only hints. She was a photographer, which you probably already know. She never married (or not that she told me, anyway), but she travelled the world. It was what she had dreamed of as a girl, so perhaps it was a good life. But like I said, there was always this core of unexplained sadness at her centre. I suppose now we'll never know.'

Emma flashed a questioning glance to Andy but the answer in his look said, *Not yet*, and she was glad, not quite ready to share the diary with anyone else, not even Ruby, who had been Isobel's friend. She wanted to read the rest of it first and discover, if she could, the link that ran between them.

The musicians took their places on the little platform in the corner and the chatter in the pub subsided to a murmur as all heads turned towards them. Then the music began and there was no chance to ask Ruby any more.

It was a good night. She ended up dancing with Andy, surprised and delighted by his skill as he spun and twirled her, her own hesitation and awkwardness held at bay by the influence of a couple of glasses of beer and the pleasure of his company. It was the first time in months she had simply relaxed and enjoyed herself, and there was no shadow of Jamie to ruin it.

Later, when the band had finished for the night and the pub

began to empty into the summer night, she wandered home with Andy.

'Thanks for inviting me out,' she said, when they reached his gate. 'I had a lovely time.'

'My pleasure. We should do it again,' he said. Then he turned to her quickly. 'Only if you'd like, that is – I don't want to be an annoying neighbour …'

She nodded and lowered her head away to hide the smile and flush of pleasure that coloured her cheeks. Then they paused, both hesitating, uncertain in the new understanding that had passed between them, until Andy let out a nervous laugh.

'I'll see you around. Good night.'

''Night,' she replied. 'And thank you. I had a great night.'

But she did not turn away, standing instead at the gate to watch him to the door. Then, once he was inside and the door had closed behind him, she walked along the lane to her own house with a smile on her face that she could not have suppressed for a million pounds.

Chapter Seven

ISOBEL

January 1944

He came back.

The next day. He came back to see me again.

Matthew.

He came alone this time and so I wondered if he was supposed to be off the base but I didn't like to ask, and he hung around the shop for a while reading magazines from the rack and ignoring pointed looks from Mrs Mackie. In the end she sent me home early, and we almost fell out of the door with relief into the bitter afternoon outside. It was nearly dark, the winter evening already closing in and the sky bright and clear overhead, the high street lit silver by a bright half-moon.

'A good night for flying,' I said.

Matt glanced up at the sky and nodded. 'I don't know how the British guys do it – flying at night. Give me daylight any time – at least you can see what's coming at you.'

We stood close together in the road for a moment.

'Can you walk with me back to the base?' he said.

'Are you AWOL?' Absent without leave, I meant. He would be charged if he was caught. I shuddered and not from the cold, but Matt only shrugged.

'I wanted to see you, and it's only for a couple of hours. The other guys will cover for me. Don't worry.' He smiled, but I worried for him just the same.

We started walking, strolling really. Neither of us said it but both of us wanted the journey to last as long as it could in spite of the cold and the risk to Matt. The silence stretched but it was comfortable, and I was surprised by how easy it was to be with him. It never even crossed my mind to worry about my hair or my clothes, my lack of curves – things that had almost crippled me with shyness in the past. We fell into step, walking close, side by side but not quite touching, and our shadows bobbed alongside us on the moonlit road.

'Where are you from?' I asked after a while.

'I was born in Boston,' he said, 'but we moved to California when I was ten. My dad got a new job – he's an academic, teaches history at university.'

'Ancient history?' I had once dreamed of studying Classics at university myself, but the war had put those hopes on hold.

'Early Modern,' Matt answered. 'I know a great deal about Tudor and Stuart England, and the settlement of America …' He turned to me and grinned. 'Family dinners tend to be history lessons.'

'Sounds fascinating. Far more interesting than our family dinners, especially now that it's just Mum and me. Frances, my sister, got married a couple of years ago and moved away.'

'Are you close, you and your mom?'

'Not really,' I answered, then hesitated before going on – whatever I thought of her she was still my mother, and I barely knew the man at my side. I said, 'We see life differently. Truth be told, she's a bit of a snob. She hates me working in a shop. She thinks I should find a nice RAF officer to marry …' I trailed off, uncertain how he would react, but he just laughed, and the sound of it rang out clear in the crisp winter air, infectious.

'So she's going to love you hanging around with an American tail gunner.'

'Oh yes. Definitely.'

We walked on in silence then, the base looming closer, and I was glad I had told him the truth. Above the hedgerows I could make out the dark squat shapes of the buildings outlined against the sky.

'Are you going to be a historian too?' I asked.

'Me? No. I'm going to be a writer. When all this is done, I'm going to join a newspaper and be a reporter. Then when I've lived a little, I'm going to write novels.'

'Like Hemingway.'

'Exactly like Hemingway.'

We turned to each other and smiled. 'I'd like to do that too,' I said. 'Or be a photographer.'

'You should do it. Follow your dreams. There's nothing to stop you. It'll be a new world when the war's finally over.'

'We could be a team,' I said, with a laugh. 'Reporter and photographer.'

'Sounds good to me.'

We had reached the airfield, the bomb-group number emblazoned on a white arched sign above the gate, the eagle emblem swooping towards it with its talons outstretched. A guard stood beside the little sentry box. He looked frozen to the bone, cheeks raw, lips turning blue.

Matt turned to me. 'Where do you live? In case I can get off base out of shop hours.'

I told him the address. 'But you can't knock at the door.' I imagined my mother's horror to find an American gunner on her doorstep.

'I know. I'll make an owl call. You know what that sounds like?'

'Yes. We have owls in England too, you know.'

He laughed again. I loved the sound of it, the warmth it contained. Then, sliding a glance towards the gate and the sentry, his smile faded. 'I've gotta go.'

We were standing very close together in darkness of the lane, our breath mingling, and he reached for my gloved hand with his, just brushing against my fingers. I wished I wasn't wearing gloves, that it was his skin touching mine, but I didn't dare to lift my head to meet his gaze.

'I'll see you soon, Izzy,' he whispered.

I nodded, unable to force any words to my lips as I watched him turn away from me, say a brief word to the sentry and head through the gate into the base. Then I shivered, suddenly cold in the dark without his company to warm me, and hurried back along the lane towards home. It seemed a very long way without him.

Today, just before we closed, Matt came again to the shop. I hadn't seen him for two days so I guessed he was busy at the base – training, flying, studying. But I scrutinised each and every bomber that flew overhead, wondering if it was his, and I wished I had remembered to ask him the name of his plane, so that I could at least try to make it out and know what I was looking for. I'm so glad he isn't flying missions yet. I don't know how I'll manage when he does. How do you cope with so much fear? How do you function? I can hardly bear to think of it. I'd far rather be up there myself, the one in danger, than fretting at home. The waiting will be the worst, the helplessness.

. . .

Mrs Mackie closed up the shop, locked the door behind me and pulled down the blind. I wonder if she'll tell Mum about me meeting Matt. They aren't close – my mother isn't much liked in the village – but it's definitely a possibility. Oh well, I'll cross that bridge when I get to it.

There was a whole group of them outside in the high street when I went out, hanging off the sides of a jeep, laughing and fooling about in the road while they waited. It's hard not to smile when you see them – their determination to have fun is infectious.

Matt stepped away from the others and stood close to me on the pavement. It was wonderful to be near him again and feel the warmth of his smile.

'We're going to the pub,' he said. 'Will you come?'

I hesitated. Mum would have made dinner. She would be expecting me. And there would be no doubt she would hear of it if I went to the pub. But then I realised with a thud of sudden clarity that I really didn't care that much. I wanted to be with Matt, I wanted to have fun. The alternative was to go home and sit in that silent house with only my mother for company, while life was happening elsewhere.

'Of course I'll come,' I said.

He took my hand and shook his head when one of his friends whistled. He turned to me. 'Sorry.'

'It's okay. I don't mind.' And I didn't. Matt's fingers were entwined with mine, and the connection flowed like a current through my veins. No gloves this time. Skin against skin. It was delicious.

He led me to the pub. A couple of the village men scowled and left at the influx of Americans but the others simply gave them a smile of greeting and went on with their conversations. Two girls I had known since school were sitting with a pair of British soldiers. They gave me a wave and turned their attention back to the Tommies. The men discussed the choices of beer with the landlord, and Matt bought me a shandy. With the first mouthful of his beer he pulled a grimace and I laughed.

'It's an acquired taste,' I told him, and he laughed. We sat apart from the others but I saw them sliding glances our way.

'Don't mind about them,' Matt said. 'They're just jealous.'

I remembered about the name of the plane and asked him.

'*The American Maiden,*' he replied, when I asked him. 'It's a B17 Flying Fortress. The name is written on the nose underneath the painting of a beautiful woman in a skimpy dress.'

I raised my eyebrows and he had the good grace to slide his eyes away for a moment of shyness. Then he turned back to me. 'I'm joining an experienced crew, which is great. They're good men. I got lucky.'

'What happened to the old tail gunner?' I asked, and immediately wished I hadn't.

But Matt just said, 'I don't know,' and shrugged. 'It's kind of an unwritten rule that you never talk about the men who aren't here any more. I don't want to ask.'

I said nothing and took a mouthful of shandy. In the pause Matt put his hand on mine where it rested on the table and with his touch a warmth shivered through me. I lifted my head. He was very close, and his eyes were intent on mine. I held his gaze for a moment then dropped my head away. I was too aware of his friends at the next table, the watching eyes of the other drinkers. However much I wanted him to kiss me it couldn't be there, in front of all those people.

He must have read my mind, because he said, 'Is there anywhere we can go?'

I shook my head. There was nowhere I could think of other than the cold outdoors, but perhaps that would be better than the public warmth of the pub. At least we would be alone together, no prying eyes.

'Only outside,' I said. 'In the cold.'

He smiled and shrugged and finished his beer. 'We could walk somewhere? I've got the whole evening free. And if it gets too cold we'll just come back.'

He led me outside into the high street. A silver moon peered through a shifting veil of cloud, casting a restless eerie light across the village. I slid my arm through his and we set off southwards, away from the base. I wanted to pretend the war did not exist, that Matt would never fly into danger, and that I could never lose him.

'Where's your house?' he asked.

'This way.'

We turned off the high street just beyond the church and went down the slight slope, past Roselea, where Dr Elliot lived, and Evercote, which had been empty since Mr Lawrence had been recalled to his old post at the Home Office a few months before. Our house was at the end of the street and as we stood in the road I tried to see it through Matt's eyes, an unremarkable building with bay windows set into red brick walls that were half covered by ivy. A neat garden stood either side of a gravelled drive. It could have been empty – there were no lights showing, the blackout blinds still in place, and I wondered how it compared to the houses he was used to in America.

'My bedroom is that one.' I pointed to one of the windows.

Matt's eyes followed the direction of my finger. 'Your mom won't see us here?'

'The living room's at the back. Besides, it's dark …'

He turned away from the house towards me and felt once more for my fingers. His body was close to mine and even through all the layers of our clothing – my jumper and wool coat, his tunic and flying jacket – I could still feel the warmth of him next to me, the soft movement of his chest with each breath. His face was pale in the silver light, his eyes black, and his breath caressed my cheek as I raised my head to meet his. Our lips touched. Briefly, gently, no more than a whisper. I wanted more. But he moved back, searching my face with those sad dark eyes.

'Are you okay?' he asked.

'Yes,' I told him. 'I'm more than okay.'

He lifted his hand to my cheek and it was cold against my skin as I tilted my head to meet the caress. Then he moved in closer, tucked his fingers under my chin to lift it, and kissed me again.

Chapter Eight

ISOBEL

January 1944

It was late in the evening by the time I got home and when I slid the key into the lock I was still smiling with the memory of Matt's lips on mine, the close warmth of his body, the cold touch of his fingers. Opening the door with care, I turned the handle in silence, hoping Mum was already in bed – I had not thought to prepare any kind of excuse, too caught up in the pleasure of Matt's company. But the lamp was still on in the living room, and as I closed the door behind me I realised I would have to think quickly. *Truth or lie?* I wondered. Which would be better?

I hung up my coat and hat and went into the living room. Mum was in her usual armchair in front of the dying fire, slippered feet stretched out on the rug. The wireless was playing on the sideboard – Vera Lynn's voice sang softly of hoped-for meetings. Vera Lynn was my mother's favourite, and her eyes were closed, listening. The room was warm after the winter chill outside and instinctively I crossed to the fire. The cat lifted its head at my approach but seeing only me dropped it again to hearthstone and went back to sleep. We had never liked each other much, the cat and me.

Mum opened her eyes. Even at this hour of the evening she was still perfectly dressed. Her hair was neatly pinned off her face, her blouse smooth and fresh beneath her woollen cardigan. Even her lipstick still had its colour. I can barely remember a day when I've seen her look less than her best – it's an admirable skill, and I didn't inherit it. I ran my fingers through my own mop of hair, mussed from being outdoors and the rough caress of Matt's fingers.

'Where have you been?' Mum asked.

'I went to see Daisy after work.' It hadn't taken much thought to decide to lie to her – if I had told the truth I would never have heard the end of it. 'We got talking – you know how we are once we get together …' I gave her an apologetic smile. It wasn't the first time I had stayed at my friend's till late. We had known each other all our lives.

Mum gave me a look of long-suffering disappointment. Without Dad to support and her children grown up, she seemed to have lost her purpose. She kept busy – she had joined the Women's Voluntary Service at the outbreak of the war, where she had found an outlet for her organisational skills – but her primary role in life had always been wife and mother, and without either, she had come adrift.

'Have you eaten?' Mum asked.

I nodded at the same moment I realised I hadn't eaten a thing all evening. In the excitement of being with Matt I had completely forgotten about dinner. 'But I'm still hungry,' I said.

'There's some cauliflower cheese on the counter. I left it for you but I don't expect it will be very nice cold.'

'I'm sure it will be fine.' I turned. 'I'll make some tea?'

She nodded, absently, and returned her gaze to the glowing embers in the fireplace. I wondered what she was thinking, if she was missing Dad.

I ate the cauliflower cheese standing up in the kitchen while I waited for the kettle to boil. She was right – it would have tasted better heated up, but I didn't feel like waiting. I took the tea through to the living room on a tray and Mum brightened, putting on a show of normality.

'How is Daisy?' she asked, taking a sip of tea and giving me a smile of approval.

'She's fine,' I said. 'The farm's busy as always, and she's missing Tim, of course.' Her sweetheart since childhood, fighting now somewhere in Italy.

'We all miss our men when they're gone,' Mum said, and I caught a brief glimpse of the sadness she rarely let show before she smiled again, the mask back in place. 'Your sister's very lucky that John's still in England. Engineering's such a good profession. Frances did well for herself marrying him … such a catch.'

I gave an inward sigh and waited for the lecture that was about to follow but I didn't listen when it came. I could have recited it word for word.

University will be such a good chance to find a nice young man.

You'll need to keep an eye out for someone suitable. Someone from a good family.

Etcetera, etcetera, etcetera.

I thought of Matt and tamped down the flush of pleasure that rippled through me, suppressing the instinctive smile with a mouthful of tea. We had walked together all evening, arm in arm, talking of everything and nothing – our pasts and our futures, our hopes for a new world after the war. Would he count as a 'good man'? I doubted it. In spite of his father's social standing as an academic Matt was American and, even worse, a lowly tail gunner. Perhaps if he had been an officer? I let the thought trail away. It was pointless to go down that track. Mum would never approve of an American whatever kind of family he came from, whatever his status.

'Are you listening to me? Mum lowered her teacup and looked at me over the rim. 'Isobel?'

I hauled my thoughts back to the room in front of me, my mother's questioning glare.

'Yes, of course,' I lied. 'I need a good man. Trouble is, most of them are in the forces. And if they aren't overseas yet, they soon will be.'

My mother sighed. 'Yes. That is a problem. But you're young. I suppose there's still time.'

Although I was already eighteen I was still in the sixth form at school, a few short months away from leaving, but the waiting to leave seemed endless, the weeks dragging by until I would be free to join up and do my bit. In spite of all my hopes for university, it seemed a crime to be spending time at my books when there was so much to do for the war. I volunteered, of course, working alongside Mum with the WVS when Mrs Mackie didn't need me in the shop – baking pies for the local farm workers, salvaging scraps, sewing, darning, knitting, making jam. But I wanted to do more, much more. As soon as my exams were over, I planned to join the Women's Auxiliary Air Force – university would just have to wait. I had not yet told my mother.

'And the war can't go on forever,' Mum was saying. 'It said in the paper this morning that the Russians are only twenty-odd miles from Poland, and the Germans are falling back in disarray.'

'I read too that the Americans have landed in New Guinea,' I added.

One of the perks of working in the shop was the chance to read all the newspapers. I devoured them every day when Mrs Mackie's back was turned, desperate for signs the war was ending, for a sliver of hope. But even with these small successes to mark the turn of the new year, the Germans still seemed to be an invincible force, and peace no more than a faraway dream. And now, I wanted more than ever for it to end so that Matt would never have to fly into battle, never have to risk his life over

Germany. With the thought of the war inching on without end, raid after raid after raid, all the joy of the evening began to seep away, leaving a grim sense of despair in its place.

'I'm going to bed,' I said. 'Work tomorrow.'

'Good night, dear. I'll see you in the morning.'

I trudged up to my bedroom and stood in the cold for a while, staring out into the dark, towards the airbase, towards Matt. And when, finally, I did go to sleep, my dreams were filled with falling planes.

Chapter Nine

ISOBEL

January 1944

I woke in the early dawn to the thunder of the bombers overhead, dragging myself up and out of the tail end of restless dreams that trailed away as soon as I opened my eyes. There was no need to set an alarm clock any more – the Fortresses flew like clockwork early every morning. The roar was deafening, the world vibrating in its wake, my heart pounding, mouth dry. I went to the window and watched them go, but I didn't look for the *American Maiden* among them.

Not yet.

Matt was not flying into combat yet.

The bombers disappeared into the east. They had been making the run all the way to Berlin these last few days, and we didn't need to read the news to know the attrition rate was horrific. How must it feel, I wondered, to be high above a German city, facing flak and fighter planes as the Germans fought to save themselves from the bombs? How intense would be the fear? I couldn't even begin to imagine it. The world had become a place of nightmares, I thought, and shuddered.

Moving from the window I got dressed in the chill, buttoning up my work blouse and the blue wool skirt that hugged my hips in a way I hoped was flattering. I examined my reflection in the mirror behind the door with a critical eye. I had never much liked my figure before, conscious of the boyish lines and envious of Daisy's voluptuous curves. But since I'd met Matt I didn't mind it so much, and my face was glowing, green eyes bright with the promise of a smile. I ran a brush quickly through my hair, pinned it back, and went along the landing to the bathroom.

After a hurried breakfast I wrapped up in my coat and hat against the icy morning and stepped outside. Mrs Mackie liked me to be there early for the milk and paper deliveries. She found it hard to get out of bed on the cold mornings, she said, her arthritis getting worse in her hips and hands. I told Daisy once that it was probably pain that made Mrs Mackie so grumpy, and she had harrumphed with disbelief. But I still felt sorry for her, however hard she was to work for. And I really didn't mind the early starts: I was always awake with the dawn – the bombers made sure of that.

The hours in the shop passed slowly, and I was tired from the night of restless sleep. Now and then images from my dreams would flicker through my thoughts and I would have to shrug them away: I didn't want to remember them, didn't want to think about the danger. I wanted only to recall the pleasure of Matt's company, the way I felt inside when I was with him. Like a different person, I thought, then stopped because I realised it wasn't quite true. I still felt like myself with Matt: the same person, but a better version – lighter, more confident, full of joy. With Matt I didn't worry about how I looked, how I sounded, the words I said to him. Everything about us together was perfect, and we laughed a lot, easy with each other.

As the day faltered endlessly through the afternoon, I

wondered if Matt would come to the shop again. He had told me it was hard to predict his schedule, that he never quite knew when he'd be free. He would come as soon as he could, he had promised, the very first moment he had time.

But that afternoon no airmen came and so when the shop finally closed at five o'clock I walked through the village and out to the farm to see Daisy. It was fully dark by the time I got there, and I had to use my torch to navigate the lane. High overhead, a squadron of British bombers flew east, unseen in the darkness, and the throb of their engines filled the night. I wondered where they were going, and how many would return.

Daisy was in the yard when I got there, shutting up the henhouse, and she welcomed me in with a hug. I followed her into the warmth of the farmhouse kitchen where a good fire burned in the hearth, the air rich with the scent of stew. For the moment there was no one else around, though I could hear the rattle of a bucket from the garden at the back.

'I need to talk to you,' I said in an undertone, although there was no one in earshot.

Daisy's eyes narrowed with interest. 'I'm all ears.'

'I …' I hesitated. I had to tell her – I had used her as an alibi, after all, and she needed to know, but a little part of me still wanted to keep Matt secret, all to myself.

'What is it?' Daisy prompted, her clear gaze resting on my face, bright with curiosity.

I took a deep breath. 'I told Mum I spent the evening with you yesterday,' I said.

Daisy pulled the scarf from her head and rubbed her finger-tips through her hair. 'That's better. I hate that scarf.' She smiled. 'So, where were you?'

I squirmed, and all the confidence I felt with Matt seemed to leach away, so that I was once more an awkward schoolgirl, owning up to a crush.

'I was with an airman,' I managed to say, and the words came out as little more than a whisper.

'An American?' Daisy's voice seemed loud in the quiet room. 'Gosh!' She tipped her head to one side, appraising me anew. 'Is he nice?'

'Yes,' I said, face growing warm. 'He's lovely. His name's Matt and he's a tail gunner and he's just got here, so he's still training. He came into the shop and we just sort of … clicked, I suppose.' I was speaking quickly in my nervousness, anxious to say it all before one of Daisy's family came in, or I lost my nerve.

'Where did you go?' She was still slightly incredulous.

'We started at the pub.'

She gasped in mock horror.

'But then we just walked.'

'In this weather? You must be mad!' She gestured me towards the table and I sat down while she swung the kettle on its hook above the fire. 'But I suppose you haven't got a lot of options,' she went on. 'At least Tim and I always had the barn to hide out in. It's not exactly the Ritz but it's sheltered at least and the loft is warm with all the hay.' She raised her eyebrows with a smirk. But then she sighed and looked at me, and I saw the sadness in her eyes, their usual brightness briefly dimming. 'I miss him, Iz, I really do. I haven't had a letter for ages.'

'That doesn't mean anything,' I said. 'His parents would let you know if they'd heard any news. And bad news travels fastest, isn't that what they say?'

She nodded. 'I know. But it's natural to worry, isn't it? I mean, you see the figures in the papers and you know that each of those numbers is a man's life that's been lost, a woman that's grieving, a child that's an orphan, dreams that will never come true.'

She poured water into the teapot and set it on the table to brew. She sat and stared at it for a moment before she found her resolve and turned to me again with a determined smile. 'So, tell me about Matt. Have you … you know …?'

'We've kissed,' I murmured.

'It's a start.'

'You're terrible,' I exclaimed, forced into laughter. 'It's different for you and Tim. You've known each other forever.'

'We live in uncertain times.' Daisy shrugged. 'I think we should live for the moment. Who knows what will happen tomorrow? Any one of those bombers could crash on takeoff and flatten the village any day, and then where would your virtue have got you?'

I wasn't quite sure how to answer that. 'When did you get so cynical?' I said.

'It's not cynicism. It's just the truth.'

I said nothing. In actual fact I hadn't thought that far ahead. I was just happy to be in his company, to feel his body next to mine as we walked together, the gentle pressure of his lips on mine. But now that Daisy had planted the seed, I began to wonder what his body would feel like skin to skin, his hands against my breasts, my thighs. Warmth flooded my belly and I blushed.

'You should take it while you can,' Daisy said. 'In case he ends up in a prison camp like your dad, and you're stuck, waiting, pining …'

As she was, I realised. Waiting for Tim, her whole body sick with missing him, all of him, and all they meant to each other. I wanted to ask her what it was like, how it felt, but I was shy suddenly in the face of her experience against my ignorance so let the thought trail away, unspoken.

'Well,' Daisy said after a moment. 'I'm more than happy to be an alibi any time you need me. But you should probably avoid the pub – that's certain to get back to your mum. And you know where the barn is. We're not using it any more …' She gave me a rueful smile, and I smiled in return, but I knew I would never take her up on it. It felt like the worst kind of cliché, rolling in the hay, cheap and sordid, and I couldn't even begin to imagine it. It was different for Daisy, growing up on the farm: the barn had been her playground her whole life. I wondered how long she and Tim had been lovers, and why she had never told me.

'I should go,' I said. 'I don't want to upset Mum two nights in a row.'

'I'll walk you to the road,' Daisy offered, but I said I would be fine. It was cold outside and she had finished for the day. 'Keep me posted,' she called from the doorway as she waved me off. 'I want to hear all about it.'

I laughed and said nothing but switched on the torch and kept on walking through the chill, growing warm with the movement. I got home just in time for my tea.

We ate pie and mash at the kitchen table. Since Dad left we rarely ate any more in the dining room. I much preferred the kitchen – it was less formal and far more relaxed.

'You were late home,' Mum said.

'I went back to Daisy's after work,' I said. 'I left my scarf there yesterday.' The lie slid off my tongue with surprising ease. It was a new skill I was developing – I had never had much need to cover my tracks before. Guilt eddied through me and briefly I considered telling her the truth. But I let the thought go straight away. I knew what she thought about Americans – brash, entitled, uncouth. She would forbid me to see him again and there would be a horrible row. I would have to own up eventually, but not yet. Not yet.

'Back to school next week,' my mother said. 'Do you have any studying to do?'

'Some,' I admitted. 'But they didn't give us much homework, and I've already done most of it.' I was a diligent student, and I liked to get my work done early – I hated having it hanging over me, waiting. It was a great source of my pride to my mother, who liked to tell everyone how well I was doing in my studies. She was going to be appalled when I told her I was going to join up instead of going to university – I had not yet allowed myself to think about the arguments.

'Well, you go and finish it up, and I'll clean up here.'

A fresh rush of guilt flushed through me. 'Thank you,' I said, and left the table.

In my bedroom I turned on the little lamp on my desk and opened my books. I had an essay on *Romeo and Juliet* to finish and I ran my eyes across the familiar lines that I loved.

My bounty is as boundless as the sea, my love as deep, the more I give to thee, the more I have, for both are infinite.

I smiled in recognition of the feeling, and my thoughts drifted from the page towards Matt, wondering when I would see him again. In the cold room a new warmth fluttered through me and though I tried to force my attention back to my books, the words kept sliding out of focus, every fibre and every thought in my being wanting only to think of Matt.

Chapter Ten

ISOBEL

January 1944

For the next few days I left the shop as late as I could, finding last-minute tasks to do just before closing and dawdling home in the dark of the late afternoon just in case Matt came. But I didn't see him. I finished my essay on *Romeo and Juliet* without enthusiasm. It was not up to my usual standard, but for the first time in my life I really didn't care. University seemed such a far-off possibility now, such an irrelevance in a world so ravaged by war, that I wondered if I would ever get there after all and whether it even mattered if I did or not.

On Monday evening I stepped out of the shop into the high street and shivered as the chill stung against my cheeks. The cold snap showed no signs of letting up, and I hunched my shoulders against it, hands deep in the pockets of my coat, collar turned high as I glanced along the high street, still hoping, before I set off home with reluctance.

I was beginning to wonder if Matt would ever come again, or

if I had only imagined the feeling between us and he had forgotten me already, lost interest. I didn't want to believe it. Four days ago I was convinced I'd found my soul mate, the man I wanted to be with for the rest of my life, and though I hadn't dared to map out a future for us it seemed impossible that we should ever be apart – we were so right together, his company so easy. I felt complete when I was with him, as though I needed nothing more in life.

But now, in his absence, my certainty began falter. I was young, after all, and innocent. Had I been mistaken in him? Had I misread the signs? However many times I told myself he would come again when he could, I was helpless against the onslaught of doubt. Without his presence to reassure me, my confidence wavered.

I strode home, cold both inside and out, and eager for the warmth of the living room fire. I had just turned the corner into our street when I heard running footsteps behind me. Startled, I turned and held up the little torch. The beam barely pierced the dark but the footsteps slowed to a stop.

'Izzy?' A soft American voice floated out of the gloom. 'Izzy, is that you? It's Matt.'

For the length of a breath I said nothing, surprise and pleasure stealing my voice. He came closer, stepping into the reach of the torch, and I switched it off.

'Hey,' he said, and reached for my hand. 'I'm so sorry. I couldn't get away. I'm not supposed to be here now either, but there's a dance on Saturday night in Sutton Norton that some of the guys are going to. I wondered if you wanted to come? It might be fun.'

I could hear the uncertainty in his voice, his hesitation, and all the doubts of the last few days slid away.

'Of course I'll come. I would love to.'

'Okay. That's great.'

We stood for a moment, delighted by each other, fingers

entwined as we stood together in the road. Then he said, 'I gotta go.'

'I'll walk back with you,' I told him.

He hesitated, as though he might refuse the offer – the gentleman who wished to save me the trouble when I was already almost home doing battle with the lover who wanted me by his side at every moment. The lover won.

We turned and walked back out of the lane together, arm in arm, and he told me about the training he'd been doing, the other guys in the crew, so that I began to feel as if I knew them all. I loved to hear him talk about his life at the base and I stored away all the details so that I would be able to imagine what he was doing through the days we were apart. It seemed to take no time at all to reach the base, and we said a reluctant goodbye just out of sight of the sentry.

'Till tomorrow.'

And all the way on the walk back home I never even noticed the cold.

Daisy came to the dance with me. We cycled there together through the early-evening dark, tyres slipping on the icy ground. Matt had offered to pick me up with some of the others but I had refused – I would never be able to explain away being seen in a US jeep with a bunch of airmen. A chance meeting at a dance, though, was an entirely different thing.

The dance was in the little town's only hotel just off the main street, and though the place looked deserted from the outside because of the blackout blinds, we saw straight away the huddles of people milling by the door – local girls, some of whom I recognised, and airmen, both British and American. I hoped there would be no trouble. The Brits and the Yanks didn't always see eye to eye when they met, despite being on the same side, resentments flaring, and fights between them were not unusual. 'Overpaid, oversexed and over here' was the common complaint. Snippets of jazz drifted across the road.

Daisy turned to me with a grin as we parked our bikes. 'Looks like fun!'

We smoothed out the creases in our clothes with our hands, ran fingers through our hair, then made our way towards the little crowd. I had the tickets Matt had given me in my handbag and we went inside, blinking in the sudden brightness of the light after the dark of the street. On a little stage at the front a band was playing American jazz that was familiar from the radio, music my mother hated. In my mind's eye I saw the line of her mouth drawn tight with distaste. Daisy gave a little wiggle of her hips in anticipation of the dancing and I laughed, my mother utterly forgotten. We had not been out together for far too long – the farm, work, school, all kept us too busy. Surprisingly, Mum had been happy for me to go out, suggesting that a break from my study and my work at the shop before I went back to school would do me good. Even when I said I planned to stay the night at the farm so we could come back more safely together, she raised no objections. Perhaps she was hoping I would meet a nice RAF officer. I gave myself a wry smile at the thought of it.

Three or four couples were already on the dance floor, local girls jiving with American airmen. I wondered where and how they had learned to dance so well and felt a little stab of envy. An RAF man approached Daisy and asked her to dance. She flashed me a mischievous grin and let him lead her on the floor.

I watched them dancing together for a moment. Neither of them were very good but it didn't matter. They were laughing and having fun and it was good to see. Then I turned away, and saw that Matt had arrived, pushing his way through the crowd towards me. When he reached me, he leaned in close, our arms brushing together, his mouth close to my ear, and my heart began to hammer.

He slid a glance towards Daisy, still whirling with her airman on the dance floor. 'Is that your friend?'

I nodded, and he watched her briefly, a small smile lifting the edges of his lips. Daisy's merriment was hard to resist.

'Do you want a drink?'

We went to the bar together and he bought me a lemonade, while he had a beer.

It was hard to talk much over the music but it didn't seem to matter – we were happy just to be in each other's company again. We found a free spot at a table in the corner where we could just sit alongside each other on the bench against the wall. His thigh pressed against mine, our arms and shoulders touching. Our heads were very close together, and I wanted very much for him to kiss me.

There, in the corner away from the music, it was easier to talk.

'Do you like to dance?' he asked.

I gave an equivocal tilt of my head. 'I'm not very good at it.'

'Me neither.'

He reached for my hand where it lay on my lap and began to caress the palm with his fingertips. Just lightly, just enough to make me close my eyes with the pleasure of it. I wished we were somewhere other than the dance, somewhere alone. I turned my head towards him and, as we looked at each other, I knew he was thinking the same: I could see the hunger in his eyes.

Then Daisy appeared, breathless and laughing with her partner at her shoulder. I dragged my gaze away from Matt and introduced them. Matt stood up and offered Daisy his seat, but she shook her head.

'We're off to the bar. Then more dancing ...'

We watched them go, the airman trailing behind her. He seemed smitten by Daisy already, and I told Matt about Tim, fighting in Italy.

We sat talking for a while then, about this and that, the easy conversation of old friends, but all the while I was aware of the pressure of his leg against mine, and the gentle brush of his fingers on my hand. Then, unexpectedly, he turned to me with eyes that were shadowed and serious. Instinctively I braced.

'I fly my first mission on Monday.' His voice was even and low, no emotion contained in the words, but my whole body seemed to throb with the news, every inch alive and tingling, my head swimming. A hot flush swept across my skin, burning, and I felt the sweat break out on my forehead, the nape of my neck. I had known it would be soon. Of course I had known. But the thought of Matt on one of those planes thundering over Berlin filled me with a dread I could not suppress. In spite of the heat I shuddered, and he gripped my hand.

'I'll be okay,' he said. 'You know most of us don't get shot down. Most of us come back again and again. And if does happen I'll probably just end up in a prison camp. Maybe I'll meet your dad.'

He was talking quickly, trying to reassure me, trying to reassure himself too perhaps. But it did nothing to calm me and I wanted him to stop.

'Can we go outside?' I managed to whisper. 'I feel dizzy.'

He helped me to my feet and draped my coat across my shoulders. Then he took my arm and steered me through the crowd towards the door.

Outside, we moved a little way away from the front entrance, into the shadow at the side of the building. An icy mist had begun to rise and the chill was a tonic against my face as I breathed in deeply, filling my lungs with the cold hard air. Matt put his arms round me and drew me close to him. The wool of his coat was rough against my cheek, but it was warm and I nestled in close. I wanted to hold him always, and never let him fly away from me into danger. Now and then strains of 'Moonlight Serenade', my favourite Glenn Miller song, drifted in snatches through the door as people came and went.

'Come home,' I whispered. 'Come back to me. Every time. Now that I've found you I couldn't bear to lose you. I couldn't bear it.'

'Hey,' he crooned softly, stroking my hair. Even as the words were leaving my lips I knew I must sound hysterical but I couldn't help it. We hardly knew each other but it made no difference. He had already become the world to me, the man I would happily follow to the ends of the earth.

'It's okay,' he murmured. 'I don't plan to leave you. Not ever.'

Forcing a smile, I lifted my head. Matt ran the backs of his fingers along my cheek and his mouth nuzzled in my hair – I could feel the warmth of his breath against it. Then our mouths met and in the magic of the kiss it was easy to believe that we would be together always, that this could never end. I leaned in closer against him, hungry as his hand slid beneath my coat. I had forgotten all about the cold.

A sudden shout close by broke the moment and we parted, startled, peering into the blackness further along the lane that led to the back of the hotel. A woman's voice cut across the night.

'I said no!'

I froze. 'That sounds like Daisy!'

We stared at each other for a moment, then when the voice cried out again, Matt wheeled towards it and we ran along the side of the building through the dark until we came to a cobbled yard of ramshackle outbuildings behind the hotel, just visible in the gloom. A row of dustbins lined one wall, the air ripe with the stench of rubbish. We stopped abruptly.

'No! Get off me!' The woman's voice was high, threaded with panic.

'Daisy!?'

The crack of a slap rang through the night, then a thud from one of the buildings, and in a couple of strides Matt was there.

'What's going on?' His tone was harsher than I'd ever heard it. 'Daisy? Is that you?'

He peered in through the open doorway and I followed just behind but he held out his arm to stop me going forward.

There was a silence. Then the dark form of an airman barrelled out of the door, knocking Matt aside as he bolted past, just catching my shoulder on his way and sending me spinning. I cried out in surprise but Matt was already inside the building. The airman's footsteps echoed in the lane, dwindling quickly into silence.

'Daisy? Are you okay?' His voice carried out to the quiet yard.

I righted myself and quickly followed him. Daisy was half sitting, half lying on a heap of filthy straw, and she was struggling to pull down her skirt and smooth her hair, but her hands were shaking, her body trembling with sobs.

Matt bent and lifted one of her arms across his shoulder, lifting her to her feet. I adjusted her dress and peered up into her face. It was wet with tears, smeared with make-up, and a bruise was beginning to blossom across her jaw. We took her into the yard and Matt lowered her to sit on the edge of an empty water trough.

'Oh my God, Daisy. Are you all right? Did he ...?'

She shook her head. 'He would have, though.' She sniffed and rubbed her hands across her nose. I reached into my bag for a handkerchief and gave it to her. 'If you hadn't come along when you did.' She looked up at Matt. 'Thank you.'

'You're welcome.'

'He seemed such a nice chap and when he said he wanted to step outside for some air, I never even thought ...'

Matt murmured some imprecation I did not quite catch, but he spoke for us both.

'Can you walk?' I asked her. 'We need to get you home.'

She nodded and stood up carefully, readjusting her blouse, straightening her skirt. 'I'm all right,' she said, when I tried to help. 'Really. I'm fine.'

I turned to Matt. 'Can you drive her home?'

He shook his head. 'We ended up walking. We couldn't get a vehicle in the end.'

'Are you all right to walk?' I asked, taking Daisy's hands in mine. They were cold and still shaking. 'It's a fair way.'

'I'll be fine,' she insisted, forcing her mouth into a twist of a smile. Even in the dark I could see the shadow of the bruise on her jaw.

We walked slowly to the farm together, wheeling the bicycles through the gathering mist. By the time we reached the turn-off from the road the cloud had settled into a thick and freezing fog that coated everything in a diaphanous curtain of white so that even Daisy almost missed the turn.

The farmhouse was in darkness. Daisy's parents were already in bed, and Daisy found the oil lamp and matches in the dark with practised ease. The little flame flickered into brightness and cast a cosy glow across the room. I loved this kitchen, the heart of the Wilton family, where they laughed and bickered and loved together. I had always been welcome, accepted as part of the family right from the earliest days of my friendship with Daisy in the first year of primary school. My own parents had looked down on the Wiltons and the amount of time I spent at the farm but I didn't care, and in the end there was not much they could do to prevent it. I think they had hoped we'd grow out of each other once I went to the grammar school instead of the local secondary, but we had remained firm friends throughout.

'Do you want tea, Daisy?' I asked.

She shook her head. 'I just want to go to bed. I'm exhausted.' She looked up at me. 'And please, not a word to anyone. No one at all.'

'Of course,' I answered. 'If that's what you want.'

'I do. I'm fine, really I am. It was a close call but that's all it was. I'd just like to forget about it.' She gave me tired smile. 'I made up the bed in the attic for you if you still want it. Or you can go home. Up to you.' She looked from me to Matt. 'You're welcome to stay – I owe you one.' The smile brightened briefly before she turned back to me. 'I'll see you in the morning?'

I nodded. We hugged, holding each other tightly, and she whispered in my ear. 'Make him stay,' she urged. 'It might be your only chance.'

I said nothing, but held her close for another breath before we let each other go.

''Night,' she said to us both, as she moved towards the stairs. 'Sleep well. And thank you again.'

We watched her climb the stairs into the unlit dark without the usual bounce in her step, feet heavy and dragging. When the door of her bedroom had clicked shut I turned to Matt. For the first time, we were awkward with each other, made shy by the possibility Daisy had suggested.

'What did she whisper?' Matt asked.

I let out a half-laugh, embarrassed. He waited. Then I raised my head. He was watching me intently in the half-light, his face golden in the glow of the oil lamp that was on the table between us. I said, 'She told me to make you stay.'

He smiled. 'Do you want me to stay?'

I swallowed. Of course I wanted him to stay. Since Daisy had planted the idea in my mind, the possibility had barely left my thoughts, my imagination vivid and suffused with anticipation. I was innocent but I knew enough to understand the pleasure and the promise it contained. I was eager for his touch, for his kiss. I wanted to know him completely, a sacred knowledge shared. But I was afraid he would think me cheap or easy, and so I hesitated.

'Do you want to?' I stalled.

'Of course I want to,' he replied with a smile. 'Of course. But only if you want me to. I don't want to put pressure on you or anything.'

'You wouldn't think less of me?'

'No.' He shook his head, a smile still at the corners of his mouth. 'Not at all.'

I lowered my gaze away towards the unlit fire in the hearth, unequal to meeting his look. He moved around the edge of the table to stand in front of me and took my fingers in his. He was very close and I was aware of his warmth and the strength of his body, the naked man beneath the clothes.

'Are you worried about your mom?' he asked.

I shook my head. 'I just don't want you to see me as …' I couldn't get the words past my lips.

'We're at war, Izzy,' he said. 'I fly into battle in two days' time. We have this one chance to be together and I think we should take it.' He paused. 'Daisy agrees.'

I laughed then, unable to resist, and with the laughter the tension slid from my muscles. I hadn't realised how tightly I had been holding them. I moved into him then, tilting back my head for his kiss. He slid one hand under my coat and with the other he cradled my head. Then he kissed me in a way he had not kissed me before, with all of himself, so that my limbs seemed filled with water, warmth flaring through me.

He pulled back a moment, cupping my face between his hands as he looked into my eyes, searching. 'Are you okay?'

I nodded and he kissed me again, one hand trailing over my breast. My breath seemed to catch in my chest as I arched my back towards his touch. I slid a look towards the stairs, remembering where we were and suddenly shy.

'We should go upstairs,' I said. 'This is the Wiltons' kitchen.'

'Sure.'

I picked up the lamp and took his hand, then led him upstairs to the little attic room I usually used when I stayed over. As little girls we had shared Daisy's bed, but neither of us got much sleep that way any more, and so mostly these days I ended up in the attic. The family referred to it as Izzy's room, and it had become a home from home across the years of our girlhood.

A good-sized bed stood against the wall beneath the little window, so I could sit and look at the night. There was a dresser and a washstand with a jug that Daisy must have filled before the dance. A chamber pot lived under the bed – the farm had no running water and it was a long way from the attic to the outside toilet.

I put the lamp on the dresser and our shadows loomed huge and misshapen against the wall in its light. We stripped off our coats and threw them onto the chair. I kicked off my shoes. We kissed, urgent with passion, as Matt began to unbutton the front of my dress, his fingers fumbling in the cold. Then his hand was caressing my breast through the silk of my slip and brassiere, searching inside them for the skin underneath. I felt the same catch in my breath as before, the same lightness in my limbs. Matt lowered the dress over my shoulders and I shivered as the cold air kissed my skin. Holding my breath, excitement and desire and curiosity tumbling through me in equal measure, I watched as Matt unbuttoned his tunic and shirt, tossed them onto the chair with the coats, then stepped out of his trousers, kicking them away with his feet. We stood for a moment then, almost naked in front of each other, and I saw my own hunger reflected in his eyes. Though we were both shivering from cold, neither of us wanted to move and break the wonder of the moment.

Finally, I laughed, buoyant with anticipation, joyous. Matt smiled in reply, eyes lit with his own delight as he tucked the fingers of one hand under my chin and raised my face towards his. I stepped closer so that our bodies were touching, eager to feel his skin against mine, my breasts brushing his chest with every breath. As he bent his head to kiss me again I wound my arms around him, pulling him towards me, as though we could meld into one person if we could only get close enough.

I marvelled at the cool whiteness of his skin, the curves of his muscles and the dark dust of hair on his chest. I ran my fingers through it then lifted my hands away so he could draw the slip over my head and slide the brassiere off over my arms.

'You're beautiful,' he whispered, and though I never thought much of my boyish figure before or after, at that moment I believed him. 'Come to bed.'

He took my hand and the sheets were icy against our bodies as we lay against them, making us laugh again. Matt pulled up the covers and moved his body over mine, warm and inviting as he kissed my face, my neck, my breasts, and down my body until every inch of me burned with pleasure and desire, the cold utterly forgotten as his mouth found mine once more.

I gasped as he entered me, surprised by the pleasure in the pain, but the pain was over in a heartbeat as he began to move inside me, and all I wanted was him deeper and deeper, a union of our bodies and our hearts. It was over too soon but if it had lasted forever I would have said the same. I had never known such bliss existed – a transcendence that could light the world.

Afterwards we lay entwined with each other, and the weight and warmth of his body on mine as I wrapped my arms around him was wonderful. But even so, I couldn't hold him close enough and when finally he rolled away, it felt as though I had lost a part of me.

We lay together, my head on his shoulder and his arm around me, fingers absently grazing the skin of my arm. Neither of us was cold any more, though our breath misted in little puffs above us. There seemed to be no need for words and we were silent, the only sound the softness of our breathing.

After a long while, Matt turned on his side to face me, our heads close on the pillow. 'Are you okay?' he whispered.

I nodded.

'Are you glad I stayed?'

'Very,' I replied.

'So now we've kind of made a promise to each other, right?' He seemed unsure suddenly, and then I knew for certain he felt the same as I did. This night was a contract between us, a commitment for the future. I wondered if the pair of us were crazy – was it possible to fall in love so fast? To know in a matter of days when you had found the person to complete you? Maybe. Without the war, we have might have taken longer to admit to it. Without the war there would not have been such need to seize the day. But without the war, we would never have met.

'I may be crazy,' I said, 'but I think that I'm in love with you, Matt Turner.'

He grinned. 'I'm glad about that, Isobel Landon, because I know for sure I'm in love with you.' He reached out his hand to tuck back a strand of hair that had caught across my cheek and trailed his fingers across my lips. I kissed them lightly. Then he lifted himself back over me and made love to me again.

Matt left before the dawn. We had barely slept, whispering to each other in the dark, reluctant to lose even a moment of our precious time together in sleep. I stripped the sheets from the bed, scrawled a quick note for Daisy before we left, and walked with him to the airbase, almost drunk with fatigue. The fog still hung above the fields – there would be no flying today – and I was glad of it. However much the bombs were needed to win the war, I knew there were men who would live today who would have died if the sky had been blue.

We said goodbye not far from the gate but out of sight of the sentry this time, under cover of the fog and dark. We held each other close and as we kissed our farewell, it seemed impossible that we should have to part, as though the new connection between us should not have allowed it. It hurt to watch him walk away, uncertain when I would see him again.

He would be okay, he had told me. There were plenty of airmen who had flown countless times and survived. Men who would see out the war and live to tell the tale.

Matt would be one of those men, I promised myself, and we would be together always.

Chapter Eleven

EMMA

England, June 2014

Emma dreamed of a world at war. She was a pilot, steering a bomber to Berlin, and all around her the sky was black and red, smoke and flame. Hers was the only plane, and she seemed to be flying alone on a long and lonely journey over Germany. A sudden explosion somewhere nearby flung the plane upwards in the wash. Ahead, the sky was on fire. It would be suicide to fly into it – nothing could survive such an inferno. She pulled on the joystick, trying to steer away, to heave the plane round and go home. But the stick came away in her hand and so the bomber kept to its route, straight and level, flying into the flame, and she was helpless to stop it.

She woke with a start, breathless and afraid as the bedroom slowly settled into focus in the dim light that filtered through the curtains. The chest of drawers, the wardrobe, the little chair, the door, all took solid shape and form at last, a world away from her dreams. But she realised she was still listening for the roar of engines, waiting for the morning peace to be shattered by the bombers overhead.

It was just a dream, she told herself. Just a dream from all she had read in Isobel's diary. But even as she told herself, she understood that for Isobel and Matt it had been all too real. Caught up in a war machine they had no power to direct, they were helpless to escape the onslaught of danger. She shuddered at the thought of it and slid a glance once more to the window, still half waiting for the phalanx of bombers to pass over, braced for the eruption of noise.

The diary was still on her bedside table, an envelope tucked between the pages as a bookmark. She considered it, head tilted. It was tempting. She was dying to know what happened next, still trying to piece the puzzle together. Frances and John were her grandparents' names – Isobel's sister and her husband. Surely not a coincidence, but what was the connection? How did the pieces fit? She laid the diary aside, the possibilities still turning in her mind. Although it was the weekend, she still needed to get up and have breakfast; there were things to do before she allowed herself to get absorbed in its pages again. If she started reading it now, she knew the day would be lost.

With a sigh she swung herself out of bed and padded down the landing to the bathroom. It was only once she was under the soothing stream of the shower that she remembered last night at the pub, drinking and dancing with Andy, and the sudden memory lit a smile. She wondered if she would see him again today, and hoped so.

Later, after she had come back from shopping and put all the groceries away, Emma wandered out into the garden at the front of the cottage. It was another beautiful day. White tufts of cloud drifted lazily across an azure sky and the sun was warm on her face.

She surveyed the garden. The cherry tree had lost its petals and green leaves, vivid with newness, had taken their place. A bank of yellow daylilies lined the front fence and a couple of roses were just coming into bud. It was beautiful, spring in all its glory, but the grass was long overdue for mowing and, among it all, the weeds had taken hold.

Emma sighed, overwhelmed and uncertain where to begin. She had just decided she would start with the weeds in the rose bed when the gate opened and Andy was on the path.

'Morning.'

'Morning.' She shielded her eyes from the sun behind him.

'I was just making coffee – I wondered if you'd like one?'

'Well …' she cast a glance around the garden. 'I was going to do some weeding.'

Andy waved his hand dismissively. 'They'll wait. They're not going anywhere.'

'That's certainly true,' she laughed. 'All right. You've twisted my arm. Just let me get my key and I'll be there in a minute.'

Inside Andy's cottage was a mirror image of her own. She paused in the door, disorientated for a moment, and Andy noticed her confusion.

'It's strange isn't it, the back-to-front thing? I found the same when I used to go to yours to see Isobel.'

She smiled. 'It's like you've gone through the looking glass or something.'

She followed him into the kitchen where a large black and chrome espresso machine took up half the counter, gleaming brightly.

'You could set up a café with that.'

'I could. It's the nurses' addiction. Keeps you going on the long shifts.'

'Where did you work before?' She sat at the table and watched as he made the coffee, his hands moving deftly. Fine hands, she noticed, with long white fingers. She remembered holding them as they had danced together. Then an image of Jamie's hands flickered through her thoughts – stubby and stained with paint from work, calluses rough against her skin.

'I was an emergency nurse at St Thomas'.'

'That must have been stressful.'

'Yeah, it was.' He shrugged. 'That's why I left in the end. I got sick of having no life except work.'

'You had family in London? Friends?'

So far he had told her almost nothing about himself and she wanted to know more, but when he hesitated at her question she realised she had stepped on thorny ground. 'You don't have to tell me if you don't want to,' she said quickly. 'I didn't mean to pry.'

He turned from the coffee machine with a reluctant smile.

'No, that's okay. I was in a relationship with someone. We lived together. I thought eventually we'd get married but it wasn't to be.' He lifted an eyebrow and turned again to make the coffee. Emma studied his back, and saw the tension in the quick sharp movements as he made first one coffee then another, smacking the filter hard on the edge of the bin to clear the grounds in between.

'She left you?' She said it kindly, without judgement, and hoped he would not take it amiss.

His hands paused, the jug of milk held aloft. 'She did,' he said, without turning. 'For her boss. Apparently they'd been together for a while.'

Her heart went out to him. 'I know how that feels,' she offered.

Andy resumed his making of the coffee, and after a moment he placed a perfect cappuccino in front of her.

'You do?' he asked.

Emma nodded. 'I was living with someone too, in Sydney. He was the reason I stayed in Australia when my working holiday ended. But it turned out he was serially unfaithful. I found out at a party. One of the women he had slept with and dumped decided to get her own back by telling me. I was grateful, actually, once I got over the shock. And I liked the woman who told me. We got very drunk together and watched the sun come up at the beach, and when Jamie came along to take me home and saw us he knew the game was up. I told him where to go, and that was the end of that. I'm still in touch with Lisa. She's engaged now and I'm invited to the wedding, although I don't expect I'll go. I really don't want to go back there yet. It's too soon.'

'It hurts, doesn't it?' he said, setting his own coffee down on the table and sliding into the chair. 'It's the humiliation of it – the realisation you've been made a fool of.'

'Absolutely,' she agreed. 'My toes still curl when I think about it. All the signs I missed, wondering how I didn't realise.'

He took a mouthful of his coffee. 'I think it'll be a while before I trust anyone again.'

They looked at each other across the narrow table, and she saw the question in his eyes.

'Me too,' she said. 'But that doesn't mean I never will. I know there are good men out there too.'

He smiled, and Emma took a sip of coffee, relieved they had placed their cards on the table. Both of them hurting, both of them needing to take it slowly. It was a good beginning, she thought, and realised she was smiling too. They sat for a while in comfortable silence, until Emma remembered again about the diary.

'I stayed up really late last night reading Isobel's diary.'

He put down his cup and looked at her with interest. 'And?'

'It's quite a story. Matthew was stationed at the airbase here, and they met just after he arrived. She was still at school in the sixth form, but she worked at the village shop in the holidays.'

'I guessed he must have been stationed around here some-where. An old chap I look after told me you can still see the ruins of the old airbase out on the North Road. We could drive out and take a look?' Andy suggested. 'How about this afternoon?'

'I'd love that.'

'Better than weeding?'

'Definitely.'

It was turning out to be a very good day.

Chapter Twelve

ISOBEL

January 1944

On Monday I woke to the familiar roar of the bombers and lay motionless in bed, lost in the vibration, the thunder overwhelming. How many times had I lain here like this, consumed by the hellish din, the noise of war? Too many to count. Then I remembered that for the first time Matt was among them and my whole body contracted with dread. Springing out of bed I ran to the window, throwing it open to the icy dawn to watch the formation go. I leaned out as far as I dared, peering up at the Fortress's bellies, so close overhead that in the daylight I could have seen every rivet.

My hair blew back in the wash and I tried desperately to make out the names, but there were too many and it was too dark to see much more than the hulking shapes of them. I waved regardless, in case he could see me, pale in my nightdress, my blonde hair blowing like a flag. He would be in the little plexiglas dome in the bomber's tail, looking back. How would it feel, I wondered again, to fly towards such danger, the possibility of death? I marvelled at every man, and every woman, who put their life on the line day after day to fight this war, who risked everything in the battle. I watched the formation until the last bomber was out of sight, the thunder reduced to a drone, dwindling into silence, and was ashamed of my fear.

That morning at school the study no longer held my interest and I struggled to listen in class, to focus on my reading. I was desperate to leave, to join up and do my bit. I wanted to be helping in any way I could. It seemed absurd to be studying Shakespeare and Tudor history when the world was on fire. Those things were important. Of course they were. But they could wait. If we didn't stop the Nazis, who knew if we would even be allowed to read Shakespeare any more?

I gazed out of the classroom window at the sky beyond. It was grey with a blanket of cloud that sailed briskly in the breeze. Matt was out there somewhere in that sky and, though I tried to raise a connection between us across the ether, I could feel nothing. I could only wait for the bombers to return and hope.

The teacher called my attention back to the topic at hand for the umpteenth time, frustrated and surprised by my dreaming. I was one of her star pupils, destined for a scholarship at Oxford. Mum wasn't going to be the only one who was disappointed when I announced I was joining up.

The day finished at last and while the other girls filed out, lively with chatter, I dawdled to the bus stop behind them and sat alone. When the bus came at last and set off on its tortuous journey through the narrow lanes towards Little Sutton, lurching across the potholes and jarring through my bones, I stared out of the window at the barren winter landscape that was the only world I had ever known.

For the first time in my life I felt out of place here, desperate for more. I wasn't even sure if I would make it to the end of the term, if I could face the exams. I was no longer the same person I had been last year. School and study had been my world, my only world – and even with the airmen living so near, the war itself had still been far away, my life going on more or less untouched. But it had become a reality now, close to home, terrifying in its nearness.

I could just leave school, I thought, and to hell with the exams. I could take the day off and sign up tomorrow if I wanted. I was already eighteen and I needed no one's permission. I could be officially in service by the end of the week, a member of the Women's Auxiliary Air Force. I pictured myself in the smart blue uniform, working at an airbase, involved in important work for the war. It would give me something to write about to Dad, something that would make him proud of me. However much he wanted me to go to university, what father wouldn't be proud of a daughter who followed in his footsteps into the forces?

But there were two reasons I knew I wouldn't do it – pride and love. I couldn't bring myself to give up on something I had worked so hard for all my life. One day the war would end, and university would be a possibility again. I needed to pass the exams so that I could take the chance when it came. It was just one more term of study after all, a few more months. And then there was Matt. If I joined up I would be sent away to who knew where? How would we see each other then? How could we be together?

Shaking my head to settle the thoughts that were rattling inside it, I lifted my eyes skyward again, scanning the clouds, waiting, listening for the familiar drone. It must have been a long trip today, I thought, the bombers still not returned. Had they gone all the way to Berlin? I hoped not. The familiar fear tightened in my chest again, gripping at my breath. However many times I told myself he'd be okay as he had promised, I could not make myself believe it.

I had just got off the bus at the end of the high street in

Little Sutton when a low distant drone announced the approach of the bombers at last. Halting in the road, I peered into the eastern sky where the light was already beginning to fade, and when a tractor rumbled past I had to step onto the footpath out of its way. The driver smiled and raised her hand in thanks – one of the land girls I recognised vaguely from one of the farms at the edge of the village. I nodded back to her then raised my head again to the clouds, scanning desperately, willing them home.

The drone swelled into the customary thunder, the world starting to tremble. As the first Flying Fortress loomed into view I strained to see the emblem on its nose, searching for the *American Maiden*, and the painting of the woman that Matt had described. Other planes quickly followed, and I saw with dismay the jagged holes in their bodies and the engines that were trailing smoke. The broken tails and wings and propellors that no longer turned. I could hear the ragged stutter of failing motors, and the clunk of landing gear being engaged. I wanted to run to the base, to wait for him there, but there was no point – I would discover nothing that way. Matt would come to me when he could and all I could do was wait.

I watched until the last bomber had landed, its engine silenced, and peace settled once more across the village. Then, with a long low outward breath to calm my racing heart, I set off towards home.

For two days I heard nothing. The bombers came and went, marking the passing of the days, and still he didn't come. Fear trailed alongside me at every moment of the day. I couldn't study, couldn't sleep. Mum and my teachers began to lose patience with my distractedness. But I couldn't help it.

On Wednesday I had not long got home from school when there was a knock at the door.

'Can you get that, Isobel?' my mother called from the kitchen. 'I'm covered in pastry.'

I sighed and opened the door without interest, expecting a neighbour or a delivery man, so I was not prepared when I saw an American airman on the step, neat in uniform, his cap tucked under his arm. He looked like an officer, though I didn't know enough to be sure, and he had a kind face, hazel eyes meeting mine with confidence.

'Miss Landon?'

I nodded, too surprised by his appearance to suspect the reason for it.

'I'm First Lieutenant Thomas Blake,' he said. 'And I'm the pilot of the *American Maiden.*'

I stared, surprise transmuting into shock as understanding spread through my mind like a poison. I had to tense every muscle in my body to stop myself from staggering under its weight.

'May I come in?' His voice was soft, and I knew my mother wouldn't have heard him yet. I swallowed and glanced over my shoulder into the house before I shook my head.

'Can we talk outside?' I managed to say, and reached for my coat on the hook by the door.

'Sure.' He stepped back to let me past and we walked side by side along the path and into the lane. When we were out of sight of the house behind the shelter of the hedge I stopped and turned towards him. He gave me a small smile that was crooked. I knew who he was. Matt had told me about all of the crew, and I knew that he loved and respected this man most of all.

'This is really hard to say.' He looked away for a moment, eyes searching for inspiration at the far end of the lane before he turned back and met my gaze at last. Then he held it, intent, and I could not tear my eyes away.

'You and Matthew …' he began, then stopped for a moment before he started again. 'Matthew told me a little about you. I know you were close. I have bad news. Matthew was killed on Monday. We got hit by some flak and the tail got the worst of it …' He trailed off.

'His first time out …' I whispered, lowering my head and staring at the frozen mud at our feet. It was all I could think of to say, my thoughts numb, my mind refusing to work. My body seemed to belong to someone else.

'I know,' he was saying. 'There's going to be a funeral at the church here tomorrow. The padre will lead a service. One o'clock.'

His voice was gentle and afterwards I understood that he didn't have to come and tell me, that it was a kindness on his part. I was nothing. A nobody. I had no claim on Matt beyond the promise we had made to each other that night at the farm.

The American reached into the pocket of his tunic and drew out a photograph. 'This was in his things. It should really go back to his family, but I figured you would want it more. I'm sure his folks have other pictures to remember him by.'

I put out my hand and took the picture from him but I couldn't look at it. My eyes were too full of tears, blind.

He lifted his hand and touched my arm in a gesture of comfort. 'I'm real sorry,' he said.

I nodded and swallowed down the gathering tears. 'Thank you for coming,' I managed to whisper. 'And for the photograph.'

'You're welcome,' he murmured. 'It's the least I could do.' He raised his cap to his head and straightened it into place. He looked very smart and handsome, and I thought it was a strange thing to notice, surprised by my detachment. Then he looked at me again. 'For what it's worth,' he said, 'he was crazy about you. He told one of the other guys that after the war he was going to marry you and take you back to California.'

I was silent. Tears were too close to the surface to risk even a single word, but I nodded my thanks, and I think he understood.

'I'll see you tomorrow,' he said then, 'at the funeral.'

'Tomorrow,' I said, but I'm not sure the word left my lips.

I watched him stride away up the lane and when he had disappeared around the corner, I clutched the photo to my chest and ran inside to my room where I locked the door behind me and allowed the tears to fall unchecked.

The next day Daisy came with me to the funeral and held me while I watched the men from his crew lower his body into the hard dark ground. I was barely aware of the words that were spoken, the men who offered me their condolences, and afterwards I couldn't recall a single face except for Thomas Blake, who I suspect I will remember to the end of my days. The crooked smile as he delivered the news that almost broke me, and the intense kind eyes that held mine and kept me steady when the world seemed to fall away.

Afterwards I stayed with Daisy, and though Mum fretted about my homework so soon after term had begun when I told her, there was no reason for her to suspect anything. I had stayed with Daisy on and off my whole life. That she failed to notice my distress was a nothing short of a miracle. My eyes were red from crying, my face pale from lack of sleep. I told her I wasn't sleeping well, that I was worried about the upcoming mock exams, and she seemed to believe me.

Daisy's parents accepted my presence without question, and when my friend told them that the man I was keen on had been killed, they released their daughter from her duties on the farm to be with me. Their kindness meant the world – I don't know how I would have got through those days without it.

'I'm going to join up,' I told Daisy, the night after the funeral. We were in her bedroom in the little window seat gazing out at the stars. I was sleeping in her room, unable to bring myself to even open the door of my usual room in the attic. 'I'm going to leave school for the air force.'

'What about university?' Daisy answered.

'What about it?'

'It's what you've always wanted to do. Always. And you're so close to it. Just a few more months.'

'It doesn't matter any more. What good are literature and history if the Nazis win? I need to do my bit. Matt gave his life in the struggle. Giving up university doesn't seem like much of a sacrifice.'

'The war won't go on forever,' Daisy persisted. 'You can go to university then. But only if you finish school. You'll regret it if you leave, I know you will. You don't care now because you're grieving, but you will. You will.'

'I don't think so,' I replied.

'Please, just wait a little bit longer before you do anything stupid? Please, just promise me you'll give it another month at least?'

I made a grudging promise but I had already made up my mind.

Four more weeks, and I was joining up.

Chapter Thirteen

ISOBEL

I went back to school and if Mrs Truss noticed anything amiss she kept it to herself. I took my place among the chattering girls and smiled and pretended that my world was still turning as we studied our literature and history and the science that I hated. But all of it seemed irrelevant – even Shakespeare, which I loved.

As the days counted down to the end of the month I had promised Daisy, the mock exams began to loom and, in spite of my intentions, I couldn't help but study hard. It went against my nature not to do my best, and my pride was involved. I cherished my intellect, couldn't bear for anyone to think I wasn't clever. So I applied myself to my books, and in the daytime it proved to be a good distraction from my grief. But in the night, the void at the heart of me would open up again, and I would spend the hours in sleepless tears of sorrow.

The exams came and went, and still I hadn't joined up.

Then something else happened that threw all my plans into utter disarray: I realised I was pregnant. There had been signs across the last few weeks – a period that didn't come, nausea in the mornings, tender breasts. But in the maelstrom of grief and study I had paid them little attention. It wasn't until the exams were over and my monthlies still hadn't come that I began to fully understand.

For several days I didn't allow myself to believe it. How could I be pregnant? It was one night. A single night. It had taken my sister almost a year to fall pregnant after her marriage. Surely it couldn't happen in a single night? But the evidence suggested otherwise, and slowly I had to accept the truth. I was going to have a baby. Matt's baby, and he would never get to see it.

Almost overwhelmed by a myriad of emotions I could not even begin to name, I went to the churchyard. Matt's grave still had the newness of fresh-dug earth – rich brown soil vivid against the surrounding green of the lawn. Lt Blake had told me that eventually the US Government would erect a headstone and his grave would not go unmarked. I hoped they would do it soon – I was afraid they might forget and his resting place would be forgotten. I had wanted to buy flowers but there were none to be had at this time of year, at this point in the war, and so I had brought a handful of primroses and snowdrops, picked from the verge in the lane. They stood out in vivid relief against the dirt.

I knelt on the grass at the graveside and gazed at the mound of soil, aware of the coffin beneath it and the pale cold body it contained. Was there anything still here of the man he had been? A lingering presence? If there was I sensed no sign of it at all, and now that I was here it seemed ridiculous to talk to a grave. I tried to think of how I would have told the living man the news – the words would have come easily, naturally, unplanned, and he would have laughed with delight. But here, now, at his graveside, I struggled even to begin. When I could finally summon words to my lips, my voice seemed very loud in the quiet afternoon, out of place.

'Hey, Matt.' I laid a hand on the grave, still searching to

rekindle the connection. 'I've got something to tell you. Something important. I don't know if you can hear me, if you're there, but I wanted to tell you that we're having a baby. Can you believe it? One night together …'

I sat back on my heels and raised my gaze to scan the graveyard, observing the old and crooked headstones, green with moss, and the newer graves, dug since the start of the war and still unmarked. Matt was not the only American airman buried in the churchyard. I don't know what I had expected from coming here. An answer? A sense he was still with me? But though it helped a little to say the words out loud I felt nothing else but the same numb hollow in my centre that had dogged me every hour of every day since Thomas Blake had brought me the news.

'What am I going to do?' I asked him. 'What can I do?'

I sighed. My choices were limited, and all of them began with telling my mother the truth. I recoiled at the thought of it, at the questions she would ask. I could see the thin line of disapproval that her mouth would form, the hard light of judgement in her eyes. But I had no other choice. I couldn't do this alone, whatever *this* turned out to be in the end.

Scrambling to my feet I looked down at the grave, imagining the body in its coffin beneath the dirt. I hadn't asked for the details of his death, hadn't wanted to know – it had been enough to be told that he was dead. But now the need for the knowledge almost felled me and dropped me to my knees again.

'What happened to you, Matt? Was it quick? Did you see it coming? Did you think of me?'

Was his body broken into pieces in the grave before me? Or had it been a single strike that killed him? I hoped it was the latter – one sole wound, and otherwise his body still whole and perfect, the way it was when we shared the bed in Daisy's attic the night we made the baby.

'I miss you,' I said simply then, reaching out my hand to touch the dirt again. It was cold against my fingertips. 'I hope you're at peace wherever you are.'

Then I got to my feet and walked away without a backward glance.

I chose my moment with care. A Sunday lunchtime a few weeks later over a dinner Mum and I had prepared together, working in almost silent harmony. Mum was a good cook and I had learned my own skills from her, so we moved around the kitchen in a kind of wordless dance, helping each other unasked, each anticipating the other's needs. When it was ready we sat down at the kitchen table and Mum said a quick grace that was more from habit than anything else. She had been brought up strictly, and some customs never die.

'I have some news,' I began, once she had started eating. I had planned to wait until the meal was over, but I found I couldn't even touch a mouthful, and there was really no point in waiting.

'Oh?' She looked up with interest. She was still a handsome woman, I thought, still perfectly attired, make-up flawless. *A face to meet the faces that we meet* – the T.S. Eliot line echoed in my head – he was one of my favourite poets. 'What kind of news?'

'Umm ...' I searched for an appropriate word and settled on 'troubling'.

Her fork paused on its journey to her mouth, and she gave me her full attention for the first time. 'What's happened?'

I heard the compression in her tone, the refusal to reveal her fear.

'I'm going to have a baby,' I said. I kept my tone level, giving nothing away of my thoughts. I had decided it was best just to come out with it – she was going to take it badly one way or another and there was really no way to soften the blow.

She stared at me and absently lowered her cutlery back to her plate, the meal forgotten. 'Surely not,' she managed to murmur.

'You're just a girl. You're still at school. Surely not. You must be mistaken.'

'I'm not mistaken.'

'Have you seen a doctor?'

I shook my head.

'Then it's probably nothing. Probably just the stress of your exams playing havoc with your monthlies. It can happen, you know.'

'I know,' I said. 'But that isn't what's happened.'

She lowered her head, gaze searching the tablecloth as if she might find an answer there to the questions she had not yet asked me. I waited, patient, understanding it was a lot for her to take in.

'But how?' she asked finally, raising her head to look at me. I could see the incredulity in her face. I was still her little girl and she couldn't wrap her thoughts around the fact I had known a man.

'There was an airman,' I said quietly. I had rehearsed this part of the conversation until the words had lost the sharpness of their cutting edge and so that I could say them without visible emotion. 'We went together once and he was killed in action a few days later.'

'An airman?' I heard the judgement begin to creep in and wondered if I should have told her nothing at all. 'An American?'

'Yes.'

'An officer, I hope?'

I almost laughed. That she should care about the rank of the dead airman that had got me with child was too absurd. 'No,' I said. 'He was a tail gunner in a B17.'

Her mouth tightened. 'Well, you can't keep it.'

I caught my breath, even though I had known she would say it. In the last few weeks I had imagined her saying those words over and over, and I thought I was prepared. But the cold brutality of her tone still winded me when I heard her say them out loud at last, and I touched a hand to my still-flat belly, an instinctive act of protection.

'It's out of the question,' Mum was saying, 'whoever its father was. What would your father think?'

I hesitated, and in the pause she answered her own question.

'He would be heartbroken. He can never know about it, do you understand? No one can ever know. It would be such a scandal. Can you imagine the gossip in the village? You'd be turned down for university, you'd never get a job. And I could never look a single person in the eye again. Your father and I would be a laughing stock, the humiliation too much to bear.'

So far I had just let her talk. She was still taking it in, still trying to come to terms with the shameful behaviour of her daughter. For my own sake, I didn't care much about the gossip – I could have learned to live with it. But my mother lived on her reputation – it mattered to her more than anything else. Her status. Her standing. Her position in society. And she was right about Dad. He would think he had failed me. He would think that I'd gone bad because he wasn't here to care for me. But that fact would do nothing to lessen his judgement of me, nor his disgust. I would be a fallen woman, a disgrace to the family. It would not surprise me to be disowned.

Mum looked at me and she was pale with shock, lips tight and bloodless, eyes bright. 'What are you going to do?' she asked.

What are *you* going to do, I noticed. Not *we*. In her mind she was already washing her hands of me.

'I thought I could go and stay with Frances, that perhaps she could look after the baby. At least for a while. Until I sort myself out. Then no one in Little Sutton would ever need to know.' Frances, my sister, that I had only ever fought with. She was married now with a child of her own, and her husband was an aircraft engineer with good job that kept him in England. It was not what I wanted but my options were few.

Mum tilted her head, considering. 'Have you spoken to her about it?' she asked me.

I shook my head. 'I wanted to talk to you first.'

She opened her mouth as if to speak and closed it again. I don't think I had ever seen her speechless before.

'Are there any other possibilities?' I asked. 'Can you think of anything else?'

She gave a heavy sigh. 'No,' she said after a moment. For once her organisational skills had failed her, defeated by this unforeseen disaster. 'You'll have to go your sister's. I'll write to her.'

'I can write.'

'I'll do it,' she snapped. 'She's less likely to refuse if it comes from me.'

I said nothing. My dinner had begun to congeal on the plate in front of me and my stomach heaved. With an effort of will I swallowed down the rising sense of nausea, picked up my plate and took it to the sink.

'I'll wash up,' my mother said, and resumed her meal.

I stood at the sink watching her eat, waiting for her to say something else, but she seemed intent only on her food, as if I wasn't there at all. After a moment I turned and walked away and left her to the remains of the Sunday lunch we had prepared together. I wondered if we would ever do another.

Chapter Fourteen

ISOBEL

MAY 1944

I went to my sister's as soon as my exams were finished late in May. The time till then had passed in a blur of grief and study, and what would happen in the future barely registered. Every morning I woke to the roar of the bombers overhead, and the emptiness inside where my heart used to be threatened to undo me. I thought I would never feel anything but pain again. I spent hours kneeling at Matt's unmarked grave, my eyes sore with tears, my skin pale with sorrow.

When I left Little Sutton I was four months gone and the bump was becoming harder to disguise. I had said my last goodbye to Matt the day before, tearing myself reluctantly away from the grave, wondering if I would ever return to it. I had thought Mum might come with me on the trip to my sister's – a good excuse to cross the country and visit her daughter and grandchild – but it was never even mentioned as a possibility. She had made it clear from the outset that the problem was my own, and her only part in it would be to make sure I was a long way away from her when the baby came.

The trip was endless. Three different buses with long waits in between in draughty bus stations that bustled with servicemen, their voices echoing underneath the high metal roofs. I was used to a quiet village life, and the clamour and noise unsettled me, my nerves already taut.

I had told everyone I was joining the WAAF. Daisy was delighted, and though she sensed, with the intuition of a long friendship, that everything was not as it should be I brushed off her concerns. I told her I was still grieving for Matt, which was true, and that the stress of my exams was getting me down. I hated lying to her, but it was better that she did not yet know. I would write to her when the baby came, I decided, and as the bus bore me west across England and into the dying sun, I amused myself with imagining us as young mothers together after the war, our children playing together while we watched them, content. It was a pleasant daydream until Tim emerged to stand and watch with us, his arm draped over Daisy's shoulders, and I thought of Matt, cold underground. Sorrow welled, filling the hollow inside me. It was strange how it still caught me unawares at times, a swell of grief that rose from nowhere for all the years that we would never share. Such a waste. His whole life had been ahead of him, snatched away in a moment by a piece of German flak.

Finally, finally, the bus juddered to a halt at the station in Bristol and I stepped down onto the pavement, my suitcase dragging at my arm. It was the same as all the other stations I had passed through – the racket of engines and voices, the stench of petrol, civilians and servicemen milling together at the bus stands.

I looked for Frances but I couldn't see her among the throng and so I stepped back a little to stand by the wall out of the way, and to wait. I stood for almost an hour, struggling not to fall asleep on my feet in spite of the noise. Once, a couple of Tommies approached me and asked me if I knew of a place to stay, and an elderly missionary of an indeterminate denomination asked me if I wanted to talk about God. I politely declined. The war had shaken any faith I may once have had – I no longer knew what I believed in. Hope, I supposed, and love. That ultimately good would triumph over evil.

My sister arrived at last when I had begun to think I had mistaken the day and had started to consider finding a room in a hotel for the night. I had a little money, saved from all the hours I had worked in Mrs Mackie's shop, but I was reluctant to spend it straight away. I wasn't sure how long it would need to last, what expenses I might have to meet in the future.

Frances stood at the station entrance, eyes scanning as she searched for me, and I waved my hand to attract her attention. We were nothing alike, either in looks or in character. As a child she had bullied me mercilessly, telling me more than once that I was not really her sister but someone else's child, a cuckoo in the nest, and for a while I had believed her: she looked so like our mother, dark and neat, whereas I was fair and messy. She even dressed like Mum – slightly glamorous, her clothes just fitted enough to suggest the curves underneath. A delicate string of pearls glinted at her neck. I looked down at my plain shirt and skirt, the waist inexpertly altered to accommodate my growing belly, and felt very dowdy in comparison. Grubby and exhausted from the hours of travel, I hoped I would be allowed to have a bath.

At last she saw my waving arm and threaded through the crowd towards me. We stood facing each other, and there was no sisterly affection in the way she looked at me, only judgement.

'Well,' she said finally, 'you are in a pickle.'

'Hello, Frances,' I replied.

She nodded a greeting of sorts. 'Shall we go? John's waiting in the car outside.'

I picked up my case, which seemed to have grown heavier as the day had progressed, and followed my sister out of the station and into the dwindling twilight. At the door I paused, taken aback by the scene of devastation that met my eyes. I had known Bristol was badly bombed, but I'd never seen bomb damage up close before. Jagged walls with blackened edges stood in sharp relief against the fading sky, and piles of rubble littered the street. Potholes pitted the road and the traffic navigated carefully around them.

Frances saw me looking and softened for a moment. 'Welcome to the new Bristol,' she said with a smile. 'Courtesy of the Luftwaffe. Terrible, isn't it?'

I nodded, and to my shame I felt tears start to well. I was bone-weary from the journey, and the sight of the destruction kindled all the sorrow once more.

My sister looked me up and down. 'It's a long trip. You must be exhausted. Come on, let's get you home.'

I got into the back of the waiting car, dragging the suitcase onto the seat beside me. John turned from the driver's seat.

'Hello, Isobel,' he said. His thin face creased into a smile. I had met him only a few times, the last time at their wedding, but I liked him. He was a thoughtful man who often seemed distracted, and I hoped my sister was kinder to him than she was to me. 'Sorry we're late.'

'That's okay,' I replied. 'Thanks for picking me up – I appreciate it. Is it far?'

'Not really. A few minutes.'

We drove in silence along bomb-cratered roads until we came to an undamaged street that was lined with solid Victorian houses. Identical grey stone walls and tall sash windows faced each other across a road that seemed to have escaped the worst of the potholes. The car drew up in front of one of them and we climbed out. John took the suitcase with a smile and I followed them inside.

It was a comfortable house with large rooms and expensive furnishings. Damask curtains covered the windows and the carpets were thick underfoot. My room was bigger and more comfortable than anywhere I had ever stayed before: the bed was soft and the window looked out over the garden at the back. Frances drew me a bath and I soaked until the water turned cold and my skin had wrinkled, but I felt better afterwards, and as I went downstairs towards the living room, I nursed a new little flicker of hope for the future.

'Feeling better?' John looked up from the newspaper he was reading in an armchair close to the fire. In spite of the season the days were still cool and the fire was lit, smouldering gently and casting a warm glow across the room. 'Come and sit down. You must be tired after all that travelling.'

'Thank you.' I sat on the edge of the sofa, taking in the room with its tasteful decor, my sister's creative touch in every corner.

A few minutes later Frances appeared with a tray of tea and some biscuits. 'Perfect timing,' she said, and set down the tray on the sideboard. 'Edward's just dropped off, and the nanny's gone home.' She poured and we all sat in a tense and awkward silence with our teacups balanced on our knees. I waited, uncertain, and the little flicker of hope began to dim.

My sister finished her tea and put down the cup on the little side table beside her with deliberate care before she turned to me again.

'So,' she said, fixing me with the hard look she had inherited from Mum. Instinctively I braced and placed a hand across my belly.

'The plan is for you to have the baby here?'

I nodded.

'And then what?'

I hesitated. This part was vague in my mind, a mish-mash of shared care until I could get on my feet enough to look after my child myself. No one knew me here, after all – we could say I was a widow. Young as I was, it was not so unusual in these days of war.

'Well?'

John had the good grace to look away, embarrassed by his wife's tone.

'I thought we could say I was a widow, and I could stay here until I can look after the baby myself.'

'No.' Frances gave a decisive shake of her head.

'What do you mean, no?'

'I'm not going to lie on your behalf to cover for your … indiscretions.'

I swallowed, and the final spark of hope guttered and died. In its place a surge of fear rippled through me. My every muscle tightened, heartbeat quickening.

'This is what is going to happen.' She drew in a deep breath and I waited, barely daring to breathe at all. 'I've thought about nothing else over the last couple of months since Mum told me the situation, and I've decided that the best way is for you to have the baby here, but we will pass it off as mine—'

'That's just as much of a lie …' I found my voice, but she waved me into silence.

'John and I will adopt the child, and you'll go away somewhere – Mum said you were going to join up? And the baby will never know that you're its mother. In fact, it would be better if the baby never even knew that you existed at all …'

I stared, shocked once more into silence. But I could hear the pounding of blood in my ears and the tick of the clock in the corner, marking the passing seconds. It seemed to be an age before my sister spoke again.

'You will never see the baby,' Frances said, as if she had not made it clear the first time. 'Do you understand?'

I understood. The ground seemed to shift beneath me, as though the sea was sweeping the sand from under my feet, and I had to brace to stop myself from swaying. Briefly the room dimmed and blurred, and for a moment I closed my eyes, struggling against the wash of emotion. When I opened them again I shifted my gaze towards John, who looked away from me with a slight shake of his head, so that I realised he thought it cruel but was powerless to say so. I imagined they had argued about it before I arrived, but my sister was a hard woman to resist.

'What if I say no?' I managed to force out the words.

My sister shrugged. 'Then I won't help you. You'll be on your own. Take it or leave it.'

I was silent for a moment, struggling to order my thoughts, emotions roiling inside me. Then I said, 'Does Mum know? Did you arrange this between you?'

For the first time I saw a flicker of hesitation and I knew that she did, even as my sister opened her mouth to deny it. I thought of all the letters that had passed between them in the last few months, plans hatched, and I hated both of them for their judgement and unkindness. The pause stretched and I could find no words to say. I had no argument to offer in my defence – my sister held every card.

'It's the best thing for you and the baby,' she said. 'The state will take it from you anyway if you can't support it, and you'll never find out what happens to it. You know that's what will happen – is that what you want for your child? At least this way you know it will be cared for, brought up in a good house, given a good education and every chance in life.'

For the first time John looked directly at me and I turned to meet his gaze. 'I'll love it as if it were my own,' he said. 'That much I promise you. The baby will be loved.'

His kindness undid me. The tears rose, an unstoppable force, and I fled to my room, threw myself onto the bed, and wept.

Chapter Fifteen

ISOBEL

September 1944.

The pains came early and between the contractions I could hear the rumble of John and my sister talking in the room below, their voices raised in argument.

'She should go to the hospital,' John was saying.

'It has to be born here, otherwise people will know.' Frances was implacable.

'The midwife already knows, the doctor – how is it any different?'

'Two people, who will tell no one. But in hospital there will be others: cleaners, visitors, the ladies who bring round the tea. People talk, and I won't have people talking. No one can know … that's the whole point of her being here.'

The voices drifted to the back of my awareness as a new wave of pain convulsed through my body. Standing at the window, bent over almost double, I gripped on to the windowsill with all of my strength, shocked by the force of the pain, and afraid. Beyond the glass, the night was perfectly clear – a bright narrow moon just rising above the roofs into the star-speckled black. It was a good night for flying. But I was far away from the airfields now, and I no longer heard the bombers roaring overhead. Strangely, I missed them. They were a connection to Matt, and without them it was easy to believe I had only imagined it all. Sometimes I wondered about the *American Maiden,* if it was still flying, if Thomas Blake and the others Matt had talked about were still alive. I hoped so, but guessed I would never know.

The wave of pain receded and I slumped down to the floor, leaning against the wall behind me. I was sweating in the cold room, my heartbeat quick, my mouth dry, but the glass of water on the table beside my bed seemed a very long way away.

I couldn't have said how long I sat curled by the window as the pains drove through me again and again, but at some point through that interminable night the midwife arrived, bossy and kind, tutting at the state of me as she helped me undress and put me into bed. Frances hovered, curious but uncharacteristically uncertain until the midwife directed her to pull up a chair and hold my hand through each contraction, to sponge my face with a cool cloth in between. Even in my torpor I suspected the instructions were more for my sister's benefit than mine but, even so, it was good to have a hand to hold and the coolness of the cloth was welcome.

My daughter was finally born in the early hours of the morning, pink and healthy with Matt's dark hair, and I held her tight against my breast, drinking in every perfect detail. I could feel my sister's impatience to take her as she leaned in close to touch the tiny fingers, stroking back a wayward hair from the baby's face.

We had not prepared for this moment, the brutal truth of the separation. And though I saw my sister's eyes widen with jealousy as the baby's puckered mouth sought out my breast, I let my daughter suckle. She latched on easily, the most natural thing in the world, and Frances sat rigid on the chair beside the bed with her fists balled on her lap, mouth tight, unable to bring herself to tear the suckling child away. She reminded me of our mother then, the unyielding self-control, jaw set against any display of feeling, and any last vestige of hope that she might just soften with the birth faded into the night. The baby was grunting with the pleasure of the milk, her little mouth working against my breast, her body warm and soft. I wanted to feed her forever, and the pain of the labour was as nothing compared to this new agony, the knowledge that I could not keep my child. Matt's child.

The midwife began to clear up. 'Have you thought of a name yet?' she asked, looking at us both.

I lifted my eyes from my daughter to meet my sister's gaze, and there was a moment's hesitation. 'Angela,' I said, and saw my sister stiffen. 'Her name is Angela.'

'Lovely,' the midwife replied. 'She certainly looks like a little angel, with all that lovely hair.' She gave me a smile. 'And she looks to be feeding well, which is something to be thankful for. Let's hope she takes to the bottle as easily.'

I dropped my head at the reminder that this would be the only time I ever fed my little girl, the only time I would ever hold her, and I tucked a finger inside the tiny curl of her hand. When she was sated at last, Angela's head fell away from my breast, her eyes closed in milky drowsiness. Her lashes were dark against the pale skin of her cheeks.

I swallowed, and instinctively tightened my hold on her as the tears began to gather in my eyes, my throat constricting, pain in my jaw.

'It's time,' my sister said, reaching out her hands.

'A little longer,' I murmured, lifting my daughter up so that I could kiss the sweep of her hair, inhale the scent of her.

'No,' Frances insisted. 'It just makes it worse.'

I shook my head.

'Give her to me.' Her tone was hard and cold, and something close to panic blossomed in my chest. I didn't want this woman to be the mother of my child. I didn't trust her to be kind. 'We had a deal.'

The midwife turned from the dresser where she was packing away the last of her things and came to sit on the bed beside me.

'How about I take her?' she said, softly. 'Would that be better?'

Frances huffed in impatient irritation.

I handed Angela into the midwife's arms, and it was the hardest thing I had ever done, watching her gently cradle my little girl. Grief began to swell inside me in a torrent of emotion but I didn't look away as the midwife bore my daughter away from me, out of the door, out of sight. My sister followed, without a backward glance to me, and I heard their footsteps along the landing towards the little nursery at the end that was to be her home.

Chapter Sixteen

EMMA

England, 2014

Emma let the diary slide from her hand on to the sofa, her own face wet with tears as she understood Isobel's story at last and her own place within it. Frances was the grandmother she had grown up knowing, fearsome and strict, and John was Gramps, kind and mischievous, who she had quickly wrapped around her chubby finger as a child. Her mother was Isobel's baby, Matt's daughter, though she had never known the truth of her birth. She had lived and died believing Frances and John were her natural parents. Isobel had kept to her side of the bargain, breaking the secret only with her death.

She remembered the little photograph. Gramps must have secretly sent it, she guessed. Along with the curl of hair. Had he slipped her other snippets of news now and then? Had he kept Isobel secretly in touch with her child?

'You were my grandmother,' Emma whispered, running her fingertips across the cover of the notebook. 'And you were a remarkable woman. I wish I had known you.'

She glanced to the window – it was not yet dark, the summer twilight still lingering, and she remembered she had not eaten, too absorbed in the words she had read to even think of food. She had spent most of the day with Andy. They had driven out to what was left of the airbase in the early-afternoon sunshine. There wasn't much to see any more. A few lines of the foundations and some slabs of concrete, the remains of a couple of walls here and there. But as they strode along the overgrown paths and mapped out the huts and the tower and the runway in their heads, it was surprisingly easy to picture it. The groups of men, the rows of bombers, the endless traffic of war.

This would have been the last place on earth Matt saw from his vantage point in the tail of the bomber as the formation took flight for Germany. His first live run, and his last. How many men had taken off from this place and never returned? Too many, she thought. Far too many. She had lifted her head and closed her eyes, letting her thoughts flow back in time, sensing the ghosts of all the men like Matt who had lost their lives in the war. It was the eeriest feeling, unnerving to walk among them, and after a moment she snapped her eyes open again with a sudden need to leave the base and put away from her all the ghosts from the past. Not only those of the airmen, whose presence she could feel so clearly, but those in her own life too. It was time to move on, to make a fresh start.

They had driven home after that in comfortable silence, and parted in the lane. She had wanted to finish the diary and know the end of Isobel's story.

Now, she got up from the sofa, restless suddenly from too much time immersed in memories. Then, on an impulse, she grabbed her keys and went out into the lane. Andy was in his garden, sitting at the little table with a beer in his hand, enjoying the warmth of the evening. He raised the bottle in salute, smiling.

'Fancy a walk?' she said.

'Sure,' he replied. A moment later and he was beside her in the lane. 'Where are we going?'

'To see my grandad,' she said, with a smile. 'My *real* grandad. He's buried in the churchyard here …'

And as they walked through the village together she began to tell him the whole story, relieved to know the truth at last.

It felt like the end of a chapter and a new beginning.

* * *

Thank you so much for reading.
You can read more about the crew of
*The American Maiden in **Another Time and Place.***
Available from all good online bookstores.

Or please read on for a preview.

Another Time and Place - Preview

He wasn't coming back.

She waited for him at the hotel near the air base, roused from dreams by the sortie of bombers flying east overhead, lying shattered and sweating, awake but still in the nightmare.

Dragging herself from the warmth of the bed, she shivered as the winter air touched bare skin, and dressed hurriedly in the semi-darkness of the morning. Downstairs, the hotel was just beginning to stir and outside, shadows made their way here and there across the village.

She walked all morning to fill the space before the bombers returned, unable to find peace, her steps always drawn towards the air base, waiting, waiting. She bought a *Daily Express* from the shop in the village and saw the words Monte Cassino in the headline, but the name held no meaning for her and she tossed the paper aside on the hotel bed, unopened.

It was lunchtime when the planes returned, a distant drone that rose to the familiar roar, and she raced down three flights of stairs to stand on the street, watching the damaged aircraft flying low across the village, searching among them for the *American Maiden*, unable to make out the names. She almost ran to the base as the planes came into land one after another, and the silence of the afternoon was deafening when the last engine finally died. Pacing back and forth, never far from the gate, she waited till the chill of the evening began to settle around her and the light to leave the sky, before she returned to the hotel, arms wrapped around herself against the cold, useless because the cold was inside her.

She waited all night for him, refusing to believe that he hadn't returned, wrapped in her arms, cold and in pain, hating each footstep on the stairs that wasn't his. Staring into the fire, she hoped against hope that there was some other explanation, that some miracle might bring him to her even now. But the morning light brought no relief, just the thunder of another mission flying overhead and the growing realisation of the truth. He wasn't coming back.

But she waited still, unable to leave, walking again in the lanes near the base as though by being close to where he should be he would come. Once, she approached the gate, wanting to ask the sentry, desperate for information, but at the last moment she backed away, knowing he would tell her nothing, that she had no proof of who she was.

Late in the afternoon, as the winter light ceded easily to the darkness, she retraced her steps to the hotel and another night of fitful sleeping, dreams of fire and falling planes. Then finally, as the sun rose once more behind its shroud of grey, she understood that he would not come, so she packed her few belongings, paid the bill with the money he had given her, and went outside to wait for the bus that would take her home.

Another Time and Place
is available from all good online bookstores.

Also by Samantha Grosser

OUT OF THE ASHES

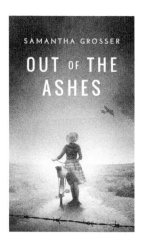

England 1944. Among the ruins of the Second World War, an illegal and tentative friendship begins.

When a young war widow meets an enemy prisoner of war in the final days of World War II, old certainties are put to the test. An enthralling novel of love, betrayal, and second chances.

Out of the Ashes

is available from all good online bookstores.

About the Author

Historical fiction author Samantha Grosser has an Honours Degree in English Literature and spent many years teaching English both in Asia and Australia. Although she originally hails from England, she now lives in Sydney, Australia, with her husband, son, and a very small dog called Livvy.
You can sign up for news and special offers at her website: samgrosserbooks.com

facebook.com/samgrosserbooks
instagram.com/samgrosserbooks
goodreads.com/Samantha_Grosser

Printed in Great Britain
by Amazon

35976100R00067